D0999079

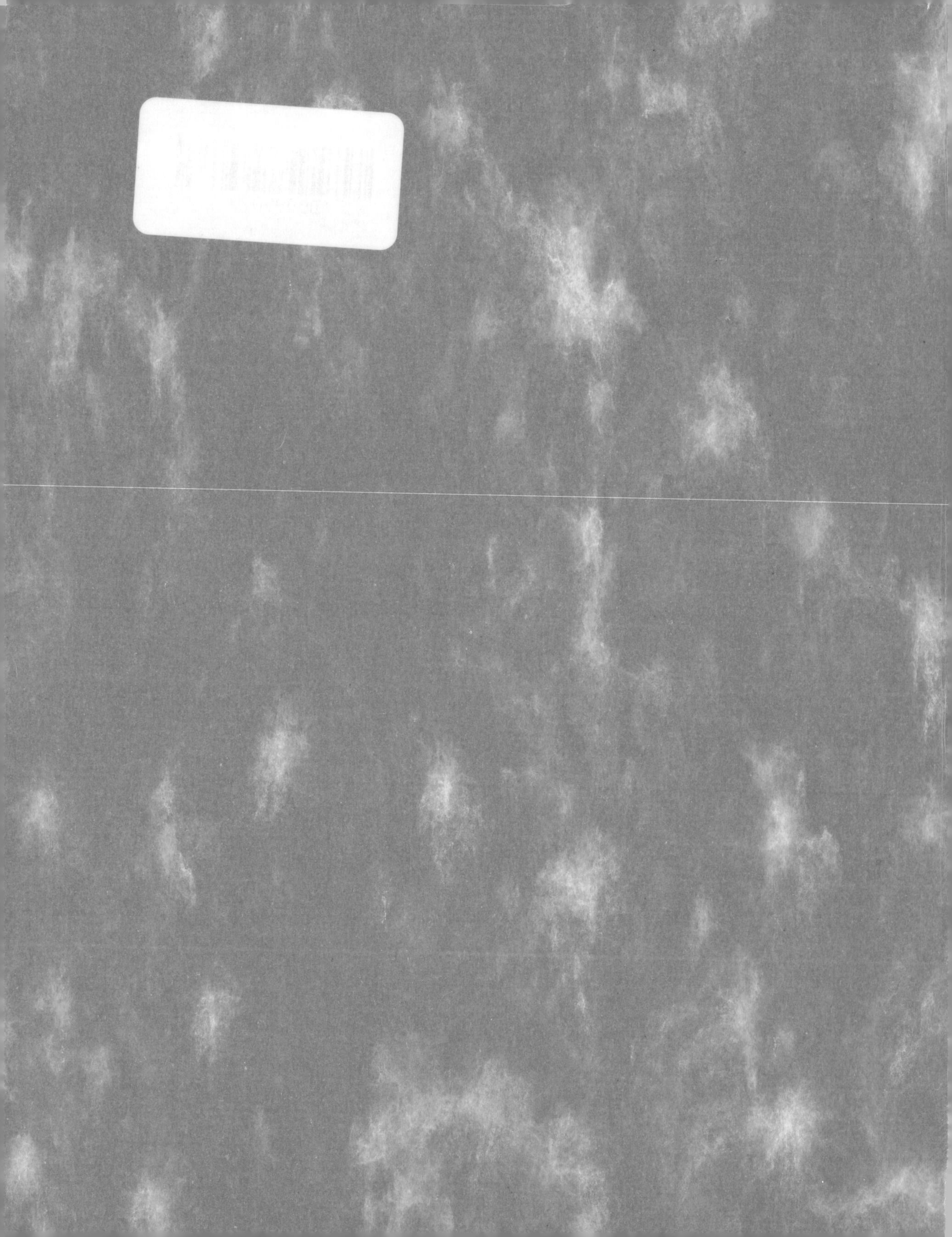

Beyond Words

The Creative Voices of WriteGirl

A WriteGirl Publication

Also from WriteGirl Publications

Silhouette: Bold Lines & Voices from WriteGirl

Listen to Me: Shared Secrets from WriteGirl

Lines of Velocity: Words that Move from WriteGirl

Untangled: Stories & Poetry from the Women and Girls of WriteGirl

Nothing Held Back: Truth & Fiction from WriteGirl

Pieces of Me: The Voices of WriteGirl

Bold Ink: Collected Voices of Women and Girls

Threads

Pens on Fire: Creative Writing Experiments for Teens from WriteGirl (Curriculum Guide)

In-Schools Program Anthologies

Sound of My Voice: Bold Words from the WriteGirl In-Schools Program

This is Our Space: Bold Words from the WriteGirl In-Schools Program

Ocean of Words: Bold Voices from the WriteGirl In-Schools Program

Reflections: Creative Writing from Destiny Girls Academy

Afternoon Shine: Creative Writing from the Bold Ink Writers Program at the Marc & Eva Stern Math and Science School

Words That Echo: Creative Writing from Downey, Lawndale and Lynwood Cal-SAFE Schools

The Landscape Ahead: Creative Writing from New Village Charter High School

Sometimes, Just Sometimes: Creative Writing from La Vida West and Lynwood Cal-SAFE Programs

Everything About Her: Creative Writing from New Village High School

Visible Voices: Creative Writing from Destiny Girls Academy

Now That I Think About It: Creative Writing from Destiny Girls Academy

Look at Me Long Enough: Creative Writing from Destiny Girls Academy

Acclaim For WriteGirl Publications

Praise for *Beyond Words: The Creative Voices of WriteGirl*

"There is nothing more powerful than thoughts and nothing more damaging than having no outlet for expressing those thoughts. *Beyond Words* is that outlet. For these young women, this anthology represents mental and emotional liberation via pens, pencils, and keyboard strokes."

- Felicia D. Henderson, television writer/Executive Producer, *Fringe, Gossip Girl*

"Powerful and strong, raw and vulnerable – these are the voices of girls who demand to be heard. Girls who know their words have real meaning, in a world that can often feel anything but real. WriteGirl's latest anthology, *Beyond Words*, is proof of their conviction. You will not only hear them, but you'll never forget them."

- Kami Garcia, *New York Times* Bestselling Author of *Beautiful Creatures*

"Writing is the level playing field. No matter how rich or poor, tall or short, pretty or plain, if you can write, you can find personal fulfillment, build self-confidence and influence others to help your dreams become realities. Kudos to WriteGirl for providing young, female writers in our city the chance to learn the art of communication. The power of your program is evident on each and every page of your latest anthology, *Beyond Words*."

- Lynda Resnick, entrepreneur, author, *Rubies in the Orchard*

"If you want inspiring, gutsy, heartfelt stories, and you don't have access to a diary — here are voices, strong and passionate. Having been a part of a WriteGirl workshop, all I could think was, 'Why didn't I have this support when I was a teen?!' We all want to be heard. I love what these girls have done with this book."

- Rita Hsiao, screenwriter, *Toy Story 2, Mulan*

"Writing has been my life and I work very hard at it. Having a group like WriteGirl is an amazing help to those who love the craft. The mentoring of the young girls is a wonderful way to pair the professional with the new writers to show them how to hone their skills and have a successful career doing so. I give a big thumbs up to WriteGirl and to those who are working hard to do what they love so much."

- Diane Warren, Grammy Award-winning songwriter, "Because You Loved Me"

"WriteGirl is exactly the kind of project we need now. It helps to shape a girl into a courageous and magnificent woman. I passionately applaud their work."

- Marianne Williamson, lecturer, author, *A Course Miracles, A Return to Love*

"WriteGirl is a life changing program that reaches out and supports young women to express themselves through writing. The dedicated mentors who do the hard work with them are guardian angels. And I suspect it is as life changing for them as it is for the young authors."

– Naomi Foner, screenwriter, *Bee Season, Losing Isaiah, Running On Empty*

"Cheers to Keren Taylor for coming up with the dream of giving teenage girls a voice, and then creating an organization that made her dream a reality. Cheers also to her hardworking staff, and the dedicated volunteers and mentors of WriteGirl for enabling teenage girls to wrestle the truth of their lives, their hearts and souls, into literary form on the page. And another round of cheers for *Beyond Words*, the latest addition to WriteGirl's growing library of award-winning anthologies."

– Barbara Abercrombie, writer, editor and UCLA Extension Creative Writing Instructor, *Cherished: 21 Writers on Animals They've Loved and Lost* (Editor)

"*Beyond Words* is an anthology alive with discovery, humor, and a keen examination of the world through the written word....It is truly delicious paging through this anthology, stumbling on lines such as those by 17-year-old Mikayla Cowley, 'You know you're done with this world / When you're swimming into walls.' This is exactly what WriteGirl is all about: removing walls so that girls like Mikayla can swim out to sea."

– Sholeh Wolpe, poet, *Rooftops of Tehran*

"The WriteGirls are woman warriors of the pen. To read their poems and stories is to be heartened by their wonderful, inspiring, regenerating powers."

– Maxine Hong Kingston, author, *The Woman Warrior, The Fifth Book of Peace, I Love a Broad Margin to My Life*

Praise for *Silhouette*

"WriteGirl is essential to helping our young women know how important their thoughts and feelings, not just their looks and bodies, are. Right on, WriteGirl!"

– Nikki Giovanni, poet, *Bicycles: Love Poems, Blues: For All the Changes, Quilting the Black-Eyed Pea*

"WriteGirl is one of the most inspirational, innovative, charming projects gracing the contemporary literary scene. And *Silhouette* is one of its finer manifestations. These girls really CAN write!"

– Carolyn See, author, *There Will Never Be Another You, Making a Literary Life*

"*Silhouette* is inspiring and WriteGirl is a great model for writers and teachers who are looking for ways to improve literacy and to help teens become successful through writing."

– Elfrieda Abbe, Publisher, *The Writer Magazine*

"So many know the woes of the writer. The struggle, the scraping by, the rejection. But beyond the mass of cigarette smoke and rejection letters exists a new start to a writing career. A clean one. A mentored one. An uplifting one. It's called WriteGirl... Until girls from around the country can access the beauty in one-on-one mentoring and a varied writing education, each anthology from WriteGirl offers a small taste of the experience."

– *ForeWord Magazine* Review

"Read *Silhouette* and be dazzled and amazed by the searing insight of these teenage voices. Their passion and talent is extraordinary and uplifting."

– Heather Hach, screenwriter, *Freaky Friday, Legally Blonde: The Musical*

"These are breathtaking works that explode with emotional daring, formal elegance and searing honesty. WriteGirl has unleashed a host of exciting new writing voices into our midst. Readers everywhere: take note!"

– Marisa Silver, author, *Alone With You, Babe in Paradise, The God of War*

Praise for *Listen to Me*

"The wit and wisdom found inside *Listen to Me* comes in whispers, shouts, giggles, cries, chortles, inner ahas, and other creative noises – proving once again that the voices of women and girls are as rich and varied as a great symphony. WriteGirl's newest anthology hits your funny bone in new places, strums your heart strings and strikes just the right chords to make your imagination sing. Listen to me, do yourself a favor and pay attention to what's being said in *Listen to Me*."

– Jane Wagner, writer/producer/director, *The Incredible Shrinking Woman, The Search for Signs of Intelligent Life in the Universe*

"I love hearing the new voices in these pages. I've had the pleasure of being part of one of WriteGirl's workshops...Now when I meet a young woman in her teens who asks for advice on becoming a writer, I instantly say, 'Have you heard of WriteGirl? Get involved with them immediately!'"

– Robin Swicord, screenwriter and director, *The Curious Case of Benjamin Button, The Jane Austen Book Club, Memoirs of a Geisha*

"WriteGirl is a dazzling chorus of smart, tough, inspired voices of independent-minded young women. Their mentors are professional writers who understand how important it is to let these voices be heard...WriteGirl is opening up a whole new connection to the imaginations of young women – and I say Brava!"

– Carol Muske-Dukes, poet, novelist and California Poet Laureate, *Channeling Mark Twain, Sparrow, Life After Death*

"*Listen to Me* is blood on paper, souls on the page. What courage these young writers have, what generosity. Once again, the girls and women of WriteGirl challenge us all to step into our voices with confidence and grace, and to sing."

– Sarah Fain, Co-Executive Producer/writer, *Dollhouse, The Shield, Lie To Me*

Praise for *Lines of Velocity*

"Unlike many such anthologies, this collection [*Lines of Velocity*] includes the work of experienced mentors...as well as the teen participants. The result is a dynamic exchange of shared prompts, ideas, and projects...The writing is at times hilarious... At other times, it is heartbreaking...This anthology is sure to be picked up by aspiring young writers as well as educators looking for inspired samples and interactive exercises."

– *School Library Journal*

"*Lines of Velocity* is full of magic: Not just the wonder of raw, vivid writing; but also the alchemy of writers, leaping across age and cultural divides to inspire each other. The resulting work crackles with energy."

– Carol Flint, television writer/producer, *ER, The West Wing*

"*Lines of Velocity* sparks with the lively intelligence of gifted young writers well on their way to discovering the power of language. If I'd had the WriteGirl experience at the onset of my formative years, who knows? I might be a Pulitzer Prize winner by now."

– Suzanne Lummis, poet and teacher, *In Danger (The California Poetry Series)*

Praise for *Untangled*

"This fifth anthology...is a worthwhile and highly motivational compendium of poetry, short stories, nonfiction and dramatic excerpts from both students and teachers. Including great topic suggestions, writing experiments and insight into the creative process, this volume is a perfect fit for the high school classroom. Sharp observations abound...unconventional writing exercises...motivational quotes...nonstop inspiration."

– *Publishers Weekly*

"*Untangled* gives me hope, riles me up, revs me up, makes me sad, makes me happy, makes me want to write, and makes me want to read. All I ever think about is how to make more young women want to share their voices with the world – and WriteGirl, plus this anthology – are actually doing it. There's nothing cooler than jumping into the worlds of these young women as well as the minds of the brilliant women who mentor them. *Untangled* rocks!"

– Jill Soloway, writer/producer, *United States of Tara*; author of *Tiny Ladies in Shiny Pants*

"This is the kind of book that makes you want to get up and shout about the power of writing and the power of women. It's impossible to ignore these teen writers, the pen-holders of a new generation of words, and their talented mentors."

– Christina Kim, television writer, *Miami Medical, Ghost Whisperer, Lost*

"The writing here, always moving and sometimes painful, displays freshness, an exuberant inventiveness, and – surprisingly – a hard-won wisdom. Some of these young women will undoubtedly grow up to be poets, journalists and novelists. All of them have already learned to write honestly and with conviction."

– Benjamin Schwarz, literary and national editor, *The Atlantic*

Praise for *Nothing Held Back*

"For these girls (and their mentors) writing is a lens, a filter, a way to cut through the nonsense and see the possibilities...[*Nothing Held Back*] suggests that reports of literacy's death have been greatly exaggerated, that language remains a transformative force."

– David Ulin, Editor, *Los Angeles Times Book Review*

Praise for *Pieces of Me*

"Wow! I couldn't stop reading this. Talk about goosebumps! This book will shock you – and make you think – and make you FEEL – all at the same time!"

– R.L. Stine, author, *Goosebumps* and *Fear Street* series

"All the boldness, unselfconsciousness, lack of vanity and beautiful raw talent that is usually tamped down by adulthood bursts from these pages and announces a formidable new crop of young writers."

– Meghan Daum, author, *Life Would Be Beautiful If I Lived In That House* and *My Misspent Youth*

"*Pieces of Me* is a riveting collection of creative writing produced by girls and women with enormous talent. On every page you'll encounter fresh voices and vibrant poems and stories that pull you into these writers' worlds, into the energy of their lives."

– Vendela Vida, author, *The Lovers* and *Let The Northern Lights Erase Your Name*

Awards for WriteGirl Publications

2010 Winner, New York Book Festival, Teenage: *Silhouette*
2010 Winner, International Book Awards, Anthologies-Nonfiction: *Silhouette*
2010 Winner, London Book Festival, Anthologies: *Silhouette*
2010 1st Place, National Indie Excellence Awards, Anthologies: *Silhouette*
2010 Finalist, *ForeWord Reviews* Book of the Year Awards, Anthologies: *Silhouette*
2009 Winner, Los Angeles Book Festival, Nonfiction: *Silhouette*
2009 Winner, National Best Book Awards, USA Book News, Anthologies: *Silhouette*
2009 Silver Medalist, Independent Publisher Book Awards: *Listen to Me*
2009 1st Place, National Indie Excellence Awards, Anthologies: *Listen to Me*
2009 2nd Place, San Francisco Book Awards, Teenage: *Listen to Me*
2009 Finalist, *ForeWord Magazine* Book of the Year Awards, Anthologies: *Listen to Me*
2009 Runner Up, New York Book Festival, Teenage: *Listen to Me*
2009 1st Place, London Book Festival, Teenage: *Lines of Velocity*
2008 1st Place, Grand Prize Winner, Next Generation Indie Book Awards: *Lines of Velocity*
2008 Winner, National Best Book Awards, USA Book News, Anthologies: *Lines of Velocity*
2008 Silver Medalist, Independent Publisher Book Awards: *Lines of Velocity*
2008 Finalist, *ForeWord Magazine* Book of the Year Awards, Anthologies: *Lines of Velocity*
2008 Honorable Mention, New York Festival of Books Awards, Teenage: *Lines of Velocity*
2008 Honorable Mention, New England Books Festival, Anthologies: *Lines of Velocity*
2007 Finalist, *ForeWord Magazine* Book of the Year Awards, Anthologies: *Untangled*
2007 Honorable Mention, London Book Festival, Anthologies: *Untangled*
2006 Winner, National Best Book Awards, *USA Book News*, Anthologies: *Untangled*
2006 Winner, Anthologies, *Writers Notes Magazine* Book Award: *Nothing Held Back*
2006 Honorable Mention, Independent Publisher Book Awards, Anthologies: *Nothing Held Back*
2005 Finalist, Independent Publisher Book Awards, Anthologies: *Pieces of Me*
2005 Finalist, *ForeWord Magazine* Book of the Year Awards, Anthologies: *Bold Ink*

Beyond Words: The Creative Voices of WriteGirl

Publisher & Editor	Keren Taylor
Associate Editors	Abby Anderson Cindy Collins Jia-Rui Chong Cook Allison Deegan Rachel Fain Kirsten Giles Elena Karina Byrne Reparata Mazzola Kiran Puri Dana Stringer Marlys West Lindsay William-Ross Terry Wolverton
Production	Claire Baker Margo McCall Ali Prosch Diana Rivera Katherine Thompson Rachel Wimberly
Art Director	Keren Taylor
Cover Design	Keren Taylor & Sara Apelkvist
Book Design	Sara Apelkvist, Fabric Interactive *(www.fabricinteractive.com)*
Layout and Supplemental Design	design{makes me}happy *(www.designmakesmehappy.com)*
Photography	Clayton Goodfellow, Thomas Hargis, Margaret Hyde, Mario de Lopez, Katy Parks Wilson, Tiffany Peterson, Jennifer Rustigian, Marvin Yan
Printing:	Chromatic Inc., Los Angeles, founders of Green Print Alliance. Renewable resources were used to print this book. As a result, 100 trees will be planted on behalf of WriteGirl.

FIRST EDITION
Printed in the United States of America

Orders, inquiries and correspondence:

WriteGirl Publications
Los Angeles, California
www.writegirl.org

213.253.2655

WriteGirl Publications
Los Angeles

Acknowledgements

Thank you to the hundreds of writers, editors and artists who collaborated to create this book.

To our editorial and book production teams, we thank you deeply. Through all the long meetings, endless emails, dozens of spreadsheets and the sea of printed matter, you each brought a tremendous sense of wonder and joy to this project, in addition to your expertise, patience and focus. A very special thank you to the following for all your creativity and attention to detail: Abby Anderson, Claire Baker, Chromatic Lithographers Inc., Cindy Collins, Jia-Rui Cook, Allison Deegan, Rachel Fain, Kirsten Giles, Margo McCall, Darby Price, Ali Prosch, Kiran Puri, Diana Rivera, Dana Stringer, Katherine Thompson, Rachel Wimberly, Wasabi, and all of our amazing volunteers, friends and supporters.

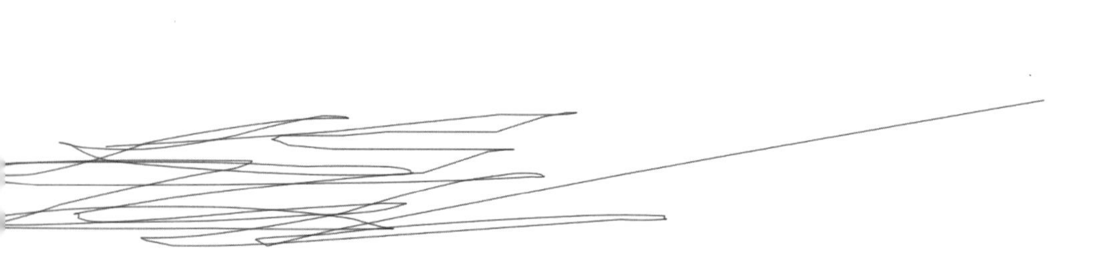

Table Of Contents

Something Crinkling and Sweet [Food]

Casting Shadows [Darkness & Light]

If You Want Your Heart Back [Love]

Introduction

Writing is more than a creative activity, it is an excavation of the self, the community and the world around us. The writers in this anthology are diverse - in background, in culture, in experience and in perspective, but there is a shared quality amongst all of them - a willingness to take chances and go wherever the words take them, and discover what lies beyond.

There is an enormous variety of writing genres, styles and subjects within these pages, and we know that bookstores will struggle with where to place this anthology, exactly. It is by women and girl authors, but it isn't just for women and girls. It is full of writing advice and activities, but it isn't simply a writing reference book. There is a great deal of creative nonfiction, but there are also forays into flash fiction, magical realism, song lyrics, monologues, and of course, poetry of all kinds. This is a book filled with humor, anguish, passion, attitude and abandon - in every chapter - and we hope it resonates with an audience as diverse as we are.

At WriteGirl, we know the transformative power of creative self-expression. It takes courage, patience and openness to face the page and create from the heart and mind, but the benefits are immense. We know that the teen girls represented in this anthology have just begun a journey that will take them far beyond the poems or scenes or essays they created here at WriteGirl. These girls, and the thousands of girls who have been part of WriteGirl over the past nine years, have made a connection to the true value of creative writing, both for themselves and for the community. Whether it was an audience laughing or listening intensely, a book reviewer responding to the fresh voices in WriteGirl anthologies, or a girl deciding to join, or to write, after reading a WriteGirl book, our young authors have felt the impact of their words. They spend time blogging, texting and chatting online, but they also understand the power and possibilities of that deliberate, time-crafted communication — the written word.

So enjoy this eclectic collection of bold voices, and let it take you beyond words.

- Keren Taylor
Publisher and Editor, *Beyond Words: The Creative Voices of WriteGirl*
WriteGirl Executive Director and Founder

Writing

Action in Ink

When you write, you will mess up; it won't always be what you want. Accept it, keep writing.

Corine Taylor, age 16

The Adventures of (insert name here)

Imagine your life is a comic book
    No real action
    No Gods descending from the skies
    No two-faced monsters lurking at night
But your emotions are expressed in drawings
    The tension in your eyes
    The perk in your smile
    The scrunch of your nose
Without words the reader knows your life
    Your feelings
    Your actions
    You
No monsters are necessary
    No powers
    No villains
All they need is you, and a pen.

Mimi Freedman, mentor

During the WriteGirl Poetry Workshop, I was struck by how free and bold all the girls were in following their imaginations wherever they led.

Questions for My Mentee

Tell me, how do you do that?
Where did you learn the secret
  of instant inspiration?
My muse is well-trained
She sits in check and waits for me
  to set her rules and boundaries
She won't come out till the coast is clear
  of messiness and fear
Then she romps happily in the safety
  of a fenced-in yard
But your muse is wild and unkempt
She takes off willy-nilly
  with the slightest provocation
She follows the secret life
  of a crumb found on the floor of a Taco Bell
She crawls inside the mind
  of a creepy stalker in an Internet café
Yet you trust her to return unharmed
I wonder what my muse did
  to lose my trust?
It must have been pretty bad

Woaria Rashid, age 15

Unleashed

Words are dancing in my head –
I can't seem to let them out.
I want to free them,
toss the key
to the locked door inside of me,
fill the blank pages that are taunting me.
The orchestrated tango is waiting
to be unleashed.

Sarah Ann Villegas, age 15

Ink Stain

Ink stains.
Ink-stained hand.
Ink-stained cheeks from resting on my palm.
Blue ink rushes from my eyes,
giving me fuel for my blue-ink poems.
My poems, full of meaning
that mean nothing to them.
My poems, filled with emotions
they can't feel.
My poems are given to you as a gift,
a reason for you to care.
All from my ink-stained thoughts.

Write during a sunrise or sunset and feel the light change on your paper.

Identity

Random Outbursts

Write with your eyes closed and see what happens.

Cheyna Gant, age 17

This piece was written during my first session with my mentor, Beverly.

Sign of Emotion

I am the girl who never shows
any sign of emotion
who blurts out random outbursts
for the fun of it
who lets anger out
by screaming into her pillow
the girl infatuated with vampires

I am the girl who eats my family
out of house and home when bored
the girl who does not enjoy long walks
on the beach like most women say
on those cheesy dating services,
who smiles just to smile, or laughs
because it feels awesome

I am the girl whose best friend
is my journal and pen

Kathi Bolton-Ford, age 15

From Everything

I am from
the red, black, and green
I am from
men like Malcolm X and Dr. King
I am from the land of the free
and the home of the brave
I am from too many kids
and never enough space
I am from learning to share
"life's not fair"
and "get up, you'll be okay"
I am from
The Little Mermaid, Mulan,
The Lion King
I am from
Michael Jackson, The Temptations
and learning I can't sing
I am from
Saturdays spent on road trips,
windows down in the old Suburban
I am from
hanging with the boys
make some noise
learning how to play
I am from
summers spent wishing
for more hours in the day
I am from
sweat, tears, fears

I am from
basketballs, tennis shoes,
throwing elbows, getting bruised
I am from becoming a girl
defining my world
And there's more to life than basketball
(yeah *cough cough* boys)
I am from
growing up, having a choice
living my life, finding a voice
I am from
the streets, the courts
I am from
here, there, underwear
rhyme, time
Time is of the essence
Can't you see
I am from everything
but I am me.

Sarah Ann Villegas, age 15

I wrote this piece because I felt a need to express my emotions through writing.

My Voice Box

My voice box is my communication, my way
to freedom from manipulation. My heart box
is full of emotions left over from despair. My tear-filled box
is kept inside my soft, cramped hands. My boxes
are many shapes and colors. My boxes
are all in one bigger box, full of words,
meaning. My voice box needs a typewriter
because you can't hear
my emotions.

Guadalupe Salgado, age 17

Who I Am

I'm at constant speed
I'm a changin' machine
no two steps forward, no backwards glance
gesturing myself out of this one, yeah that's right
I'm no starlet, no Monroe
just a silly girl
running life down
like a foreign enemy of love
A flower power soldier who showed up
too late for the fight
an old pioneer chipping away at her raggedy boots
wondering when life will begin

Jala' Curtis, age 14

I had an out-of-body experience and I saw myself as someone separate.

Bird's Eye View

A girl beneath me
looks vulnerable and naïve
waiting for a distraction
from her thoughts,
her face stuck in an awed
expression –
eyes absent, mouth wide open
she is lost; looking for herself
she glances up and holds
her gaze...She's found me.

Don't try to sound like someone else – that's their job. Your job is to share your voice with the world.

Madelinn Ornelas, age 15

Silhouette

Anyone who is anyone can see I'm not me.
I'm an unknown
like a silhouette
like the bottom of the sea.
Stitches of the dark past
build my shadow's figure
and the sun never shines on me,
but it doesn't matter
because I enjoy the moon's company.

Stephanie Hernandez, age 16

I wrote this because I want people to get a sense of the kind of person I am.

Quintessential

I am an uncommon girl with powerful feelings.
That girl you see in back of the class,
who laughs for the silliest reasons.

A daughter who wishes everything to go well,
a young girl with tremendous hopes and dreams,
who comforts people when they're having an awful day,
with a smile that can melt people's hearts.

A free-spirited mind, an L.A. person who likes going out
to the fast, loud, artsy, weird streets of the city.
The girl you see riding around in her Hello Kitty beach cruiser,
who likes to listen to sick rhymes, fast beats,
music with some soul in it.
A rebel-looking girl who people think is up to no good.

I am not perfect nor near.
I am a girl who is always looking up at the stars,
looking for the brightest one and making a wish upon it.

I am a Princess wishing for her Prince Charming
to sweep her off her feet.
I am quintessential.
I am a writer.

I am Stephanie.

Music

Listen to That

Always listen to your intuition when writing. If there is something that you love in your work, defend it with all of your might.

Angelica Garcia, age 16

I wrote this at the WriteGirl Poetry Workshop. I love grungy, blues music and its surrounding culture. I think I captured the feeling of that kind of music in this poem.

Thump

Listen to that blues harp wailin'
Tap them rusty boots
Got some stains on your t-shirt and dirt on your jeans
Hear those glasses clanking, like two thugs fronting each other
As the guy next to you trades an empty glass for a full one
Taste the smoky air
Feel the rattlin' floorboards
Shaky voices screamin' every which way
Wichita bass man thumpin' on low notes
Givin' dirty soul to the fire in the air
Tap them rusty boots
With their tattered leather and deep scratches
Faded swirly imprints and snakeskin toes
Tap them rusty boots
Like it ain't ever a crime to keep rhythm
Like you were partners till the grave
Tap them rusty boots.

Kim Genkinger, mentor

One Sunday, looking out over the city below, the music from the ice cream truck drifted up through my open windows.

The Monkey in Mt. Washington

The Monkey and the Weasel
is the soundtrack that repeats, repeats, repeats
in my life above the sprawling city.

All around the mulberry bush
the cargo train chugs, chugs, chugs
in my version of the Pacific surf.

Up and down the winding road
the black-and-whites chase, chase, chase
in my nightly Grand Theft Auto.

The Monkey chases the Weasel
in sync with the bang, bang, bang
in my dreams that aren't.

Jo Stewart, age 17

I wrote this at the WriteGirl Songwriting Workshop.

You, My Darling

There are journeys that
Turn into legends
There are words that
Transform into prose

And you, my darling,
Were once my best friend
Until you became
Mi amor.

Dana L. Stringer, mentor

I was inspired by observing young women dancing and the African influence on many dances in North and South America.

Daughters of the Dance

Boiling beneath
black & brown skin,

their blood burns blue
from flames of rhythm

blazing through veins
bleeding tempo

& circulating sounds
of samba & soul.

Drums lift this tribe
to its scaly dark feet

as ears catch cadence
& loose limbs move

like melodies
over the motherland

while they dance
between water & wind

to a primitive beat
born in their bodies.

Listen to classical music while writing to inspire more dramatic ideas.

Kate Johannesen, age 15

This tells the story of how the drum and I first met, and my undying devotion to it.

Me and My Drum

I remembered the drum from my earliest childhood days, sitting in a circle in mommy-and-me class, shaking rattles, jingling bells and banging on little plastic drums…riding on my dad's shoulders, peeking out into the crowd of families, watching and listening to a cultural group make beautiful noises on handmade drums…holding my mom's big hand in my tiny one, walking into the local music store, trying everything out, buying my very first, very own drum.

The drum was like an old friend to me. We'd met, chatted, shared a few good laughs, secrets and memories, but then I'd moved on for a while and rarely looked back. Now I needed that good old friend back. I needed it badly. There was that thirst again, the one I was born with. The one that still hasn't left.

I am a drummer. A thirsty drummer. I was born that way.

Shayne Holzman, age 17

This song is about getting ready to cross the line between liking and loving someone.

Off The Edge

Oh, I'm edgy
Oh, I'm not ready
No, I don't want to go steady with you

Chorus:
Off the edge
Get right off the edge
I'm off the edge with you
I'm off the edge; oh yes, it's true

I get off the edge
Off the track like steel and lead
I'll leave you here instead

Chorus:
Off the edge
Get right off the edge
I'm off the edge with you
I'm off the edge; oh yes, it's true

I'm on the verge
I've got the urge
To knock you down
with all my nerve

I'm off the edge with you

Jamilah Mena, age 17

I am proud to identify with three cultures: American, Latino and Garifuna. This is in honor of the least known of the three.

What It Means to Be Garifuna

I stood beside my weeping mother during the funeral speech. My face wrinkled as I struggled to comprehend the words floating in the air. Garifuna, a dialect spoken in certain regions of Central America, has been spoken by members of my family for centuries. Its path to North America dates back to the 16th century when Africans were first brought to the Western Hemisphere in bondage. However, Garifuna is not only a means for my family and relatives to communicate; it is a culture.

My mother grabbed my small hand and we followed the procession back along the dirt road to my grandparents' hut. Then the singing began. A somber Garifuna choral melody filled the tropical humid air. Even with limited comprehension, I knew the song was about my grandmother. The procession continued down the crimson dirt road.

When we reached my grandparents' home, I thought that it was over. On the contrary, my relatives remained outside of the home and formed a circle. A couple of young men sat on chairs and began to play drums. The beat of the music was slow initially, but accelerated. I recognized it as a Punta dance, a popular Garifuna style of music. Soon, those who were able, not weighed down with a cane, danced to the beat of the music. I tugged my mother's dress. She smiled weakly and began to sing. They all sang in Garifuna.

The remainder of the evening was filled with music and food. When my mom and I sat down I asked her why everyone was dancing and singing. She looked at me and patted my hair.

"Your grandmother was a well-respected woman. People have come from all over Honduras and America to celebrate her life, not her death."

Vasti Carrion, age 17

This poem was my first attempt at blues poetry. This is about apologizing, which is hard for me to do.

To Learn

As I was comin' down the road
  I felt guilty for my sentiments
No one knew, I tried makin' up for them

  My sense of pride wouldn't let me
  My sense of pride wouldn't let me
I figured I had to, let go of, this daunting feelin'

  After I went to
  After I went to
Apologize. I'd finally let go.

Challenges

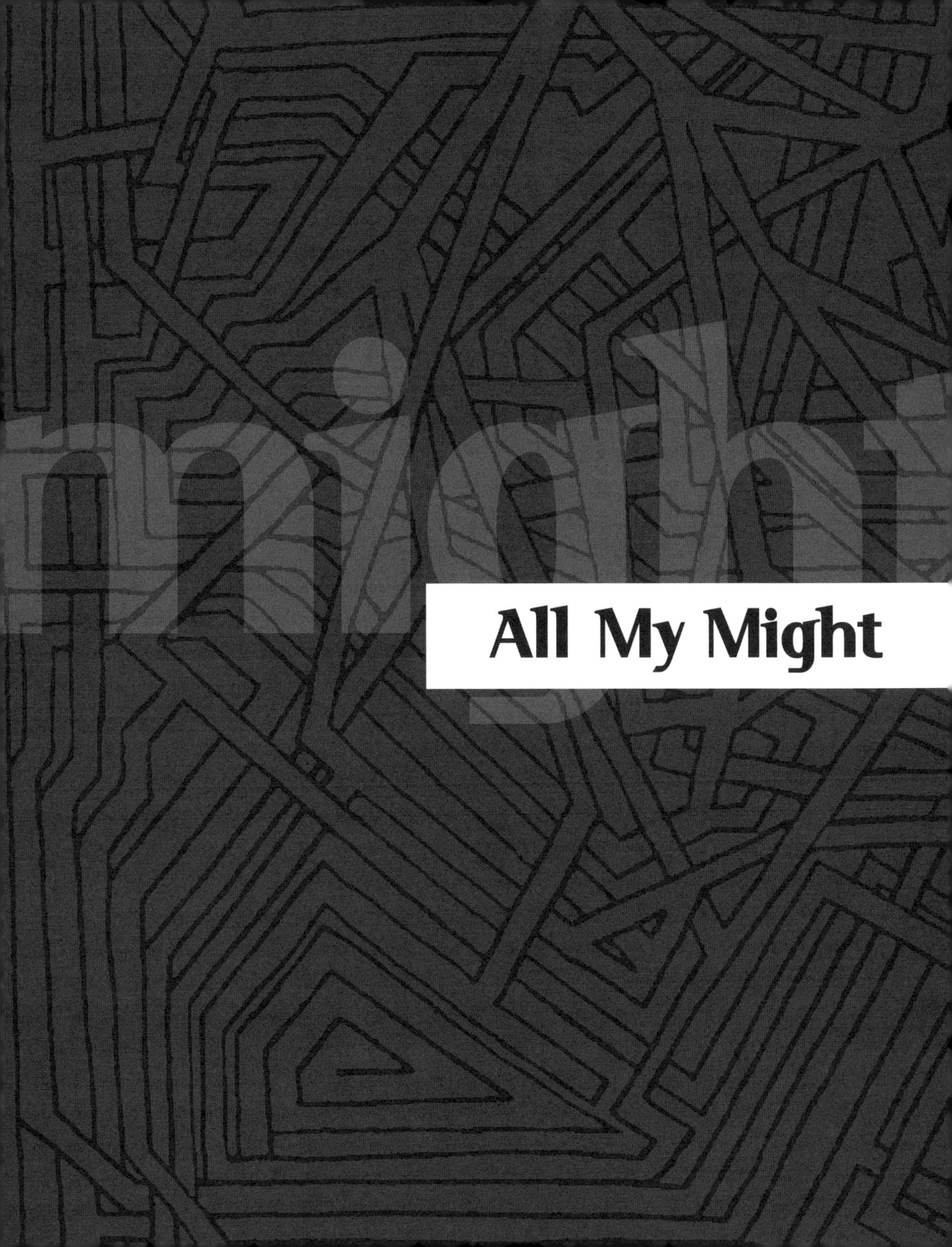

All My Might

Write about your deepest darkest secret, but hide it in a poem.

Tessa Curran, age 16

This piece was inspired by a movie I watched that was about chasing your dreams. Skydiving felt like an appropriate metaphor.

Skydiving

It's time. You're ready. They're ready. The fear takes over now.

Your instincts say "no," but your need for adrenaline is an ever-constant thumping, screaming at you: "Yes, yes, yes!" As you put on your goggles and prepare to jump, your heart thumps faster and harder. You can feel it everywhere. The fear pulls you back, but the wonder already has an unbreakable grip and an undeniable persistence. The hardest part is jumping - that you always knew - but is it worth it?

"Yes," you decide and you fling your body 12,500 feet above the earth. And you feel it, the moment of freedom. But soon enough, fear ambushes freedom as your body hurtles through the air. The fall is terrifying, but you've got your parachute and, in no time at all, you are drifting whimsically to the ground.

You've done it - you've taken the leap.

Heaven Wycoff, age 15

Cold Winds

Cold winds run through my body.
No one knows where I've been,
What I've done or how I've lived.
All they see is one who's troubled.
All they see is my worn body, numb.
My soul struggles for answers.
God
I need you to help me, lead me
In the correct and rightful way.
Empty spirit, empty stomach,
Empty heart, empty soul.
My mind races:
Where will I sleep? What will I eat?
While other kids think about how to compete
With the fashion and cars and clothes and shoes
And friends and foes and sports and the mall
And what she heard and what he said.
When they go home at night, they rest in their beds.
While I continue my night, sleepless.
Cold winds running through my body, I'm shivering.
But then again, no one knows how I've lived.

Xiomara Avila, age 13

I wrote this at the WriteGirl Journalism Workshop. This happened to my cousin the day before. It was a lot of fun writing it because I felt like a journalist.

Nurse's Mistake

On Friday, December 11, 2009, there was an incident that occurred on the school grounds. A 7th grade boy fell while going to the locker rooms to change and go to nutrition. The boy advised his teacher that he fell and landed on his arm. The teacher sent the boy to the nurse, who only bandaged his arm, ignoring his pain. Then the nurse sent the boy back to class.

The mistake that she made, other than ignoring the pain, was forgetting to contact his parents. After school, when the boy told his mom what had happened, she was very angry. She wasn't mad because her son hurt himself. Instead, she was mad at the fact that the school only contacts her when her son is acting up or misbehaving, but they never once bothered to contact her when her son was hurt. It turns out that the 7th grade boy had a fractured arm, and the school did nothing about it.

Margo McCall, mentor

I'm sharing this poem to celebrate that in endings, there are new beginnings, new opportunities for self-discovery.

Purification by Flame

For a full year I wore widow's weeds
Moping and hoping
Through the seasons
That what once was, could
Be again. Us, the thing
Discarded along with
The household trash.
I sucked sustenance from
Memories, the taste of ash
Bitter on my tongue.
Searched for secret messages
Between the pixels in pictures
Tortured myself with what ifs and whys.
Today I burned my black veils
In a great conflagration,
Watched bits of sinewy cloth
Swirl in the sky like vultures.
Away. Be gone with you, winged scavengers.
I am finished with you, heart-ripping grief
And you too, sorrow weeping on my pillow
I am done reliving the same death
The mourning period over
I will now burn bright.

Don't stop. Keep writing through the confusion.

Dezirae Villagomez, age 14

This is part of a longer fiction piece.

Dakota

"We are here today to remember our loving friend Dakota ..."

The flowers next to the casket smell of sweet lavender.

I hate funerals. Everybody cries. The casket just sits there while everybody stares and remembers the good times. Then they start crying even more.

My dad stands next to me staring at the ground. Ever since Mom died, he never wants to talk about anything. Whenever I ask him about her, he says, "Maybe some other time." It's been like this since I was seven.

*

First day of school. I don't know anybody. I don't know where my classes are. I can't open my locker.

"Do you need help with that?"

I turn around and he's staring directly at me. He asks me for my locker number and opens it without a struggle.

"My name's Dakota." He holds out his hand.

*

My dad walks into the kitchen while I pour a glass of milk.

"Honey, I'm sorry you lost your friend, but you can't just sit in your room all day," he says.

"Well what am I supposed to do? Go outside and skip and sing and say that I'm the happiest person in the world?"

As soon as I say it, I'm sorry. "Dad, I just don't feel like talking about it."

I go upstairs and shut the door to my bedroom and think of the first time Dakota told me about his little sister, Samantha.

*

"Did you know I had a little sister?"

I turn to Dakota.

"We were jumping into the pool and playing tag. I jumped into the shallow end first. When I took a breath, I didn't see Sam. I looked to my right, and there she was, fighting for her life in the deep end. I ran to Mom but when we got back there, Sam was at the bottom of the pool and she wasn't moving. I was seven and she was five."

I wrap my arms around him. My heart feels as if it were about to crumble and disappear into thin air.

"Dakota, let me tell you about what happened to my mother," I begin.

Trina Gaynon, mentor

My last job search was over ten years ago. The whole process of job hunting has changed enormously, and it's a puzzle I can't seem to solve.

Confession

I wish a job would fall out of the blue
as a ripe orange falls off the tree in the backyard,
something part-time, paying more than minimum,
a job that won't split and mold like an orange does
when it lands hard in the grass.

Yasmine Alfakey, age 16

Unconventional

Chorus:
She's unconventional
multidimensional
She is confused in every
avenue of her complicated life

Verse:
She's a rebel
searching desperately for trouble
She imagines being glamorous
on the television in your
living room
You can't control her
Don't dare ignore her
Feed her insecurities
with money and material things

Chorus:
She's unconventional
multidimensional
She is confused in every
avenue of her complicated life

Write a character you hate or fear. Get inside their head.

Jamai Fisher, age 14

I wrote this because of my fear of starting track.

Just Beginning

Hot sun beating on my skin
Running like the wind
Heart pumping fast
Like the nervousness of a tiger
Jumping through a flaming hoop
The grass slightly whimpers
As we skid past the splinters
Our bare feet
Pounding the earth as if it were a drum
Flying across the turn
It seems no one's said a word
Even though the crowd's cheers grow louder and louder
"Finished!" I whispered
As I crashed through the line
Ever so slightly wondering what was my time
But in the end
The sun beating on my skin
Me running like the wind
It's only the beginning

Alicia Sedwick, mentor

Falling

We've all been told about how life can change, in the blink of an eye. But until we actually breathe through the blood, the tears, the fear, do we really get it?

One sunny afternoon, after a split second of not thinking, I find myself lying in an ER, attached to tubes, and grabbing at a friend's hand. I have never grabbed at anyone's hand. The ER staff blurs in a bustle around me, harried, brusque and shouting. After hours of CAT scans and diagnosis, I am still waiting to be admitted for overnight observation. In pain, feeling ignored and sorry for myself, I begin to cry.

Someone catches my eye from across the room: a patient on a gurney like mine, same I.V. dangling into her arm. She has deep dark circles under her eyes and a tiny tuft of hair on her otherwise completely bald head. She greets a passing nurse by her first name. Everyone knows her. This world is routine for her.

I quiet myself, a curious voyeur, watching her. Relatives drift in, smiling weakly. They look...defeated. A woman, red-eyed, strokes the patient's smooth, dozing head, over and over.

I whisper across the room. "Is that your sister?"

"Yes," she smiles. "Cancer." I nod.

"I fell down some stairs. Lacerated my kidney. They say I will be fine."

"Wow. You're lucky," she says. And I was. I was going to be fine. In the blink of an eye.

Six days later, I take my healing kidney home, slowly, through the speeding movement of the city. But I can't stop thinking about that woman, and her sister, stroking her forehead, over and over. It was like I was let in on a secret. Some sort of mantra. A small, smooth thinking stone for my city girl pocket.

Alina J. Arzate, age 17

Cocoon

Looking into her eyes
I'm not sure how to react or what to say.
Just tell her everything will be all right?
Lie so that she will be at ease?
Hide the fact that I'm terrified?
Feeling defeated,
like a soldier in the battlefield, feeling as if reason is slipping away
without motivation, inspiration or force,
finding it hard to smile, left alone
without knowing how to fix anything,
I can't ask for help because it's all up to me.
I wish I could be reborn into something better
like a cocoon where a caterpillar turns into a butterfly.
The problem is that nothing can be undone.
Stuck, trying to catch my breath,
accepting my life, that is the first step.

Darby Price, mentor

My mentee and I were exploring confessional poetry: admitting our deepest fears and darkest secrets through verse. Sam Cooke was playing on the stereo.

"And I Ain't Got Nobody"

after Sam Cooke

Nights of cozy coffee shops with Sam Cooke
and a roasted smell in the air, I'm not
so scared. But sometimes, there's no music
or tippy-toe raindrops on the glass or the buzz
of a static-y TV. Sometimes, there's just me
and I wonder, really, if hell is a place where we
are doomed to such silence. Would you rather
flames or the cool echo of darkness, your voice
caught in the vacuum of your throat? Given one,
we would take the other, I think. But given
that so few of us believe in hell anymore, we
are more afraid of this: our hair, a cotton ball
on our wrinkled heads; doilies on the arms of chairs;
eyes failed and dim with resignation and the voice
of a young man selling something through the TV
our only consolation and company.

Brianna Stokes, age 15

Takeoff

Richard Edwards stared ahead, hopelessly, as Flight 307 sped down the runway and lifted into the air. The plane's engine emitted a loud hum and he felt as if a thousand-pound weight had just plummeted onto his chest, depriving him of oxygen. He opened and closed his mouth, trying to form words that were forever lost.

He closed his eyes and the only sound that escaped his lips was a nonsensical whisper. "It's over," he managed to get out. "It's all over..."

"Sir?"

Richard looked up, his fear-ridden eyes meeting those of a young man in a uniform.

Toree Brooks, age 17

I was in math class, in deep meditation about life and was inspired to write this poem.

Hope

A report card and a star

Universities and college

A collage of grades
posted along the classroom walls

I'm proud to walk among my alumni
That is where I stand

Nobody thought I would get here
Struggle is a virtue, but strength is my code

I'm the epitome of the letter A

Edna Cerritos, age 14

Life Turning Upside Down & Surviving It

Nobody knew why I was getting sick.

"My head hurts," I blurted out at the Childrens Hospital Los Angeles emergency department. The doctor ordered a CT scan. As the results came out, the doctor said, "I am sorry; your daughter has a mass in her brain, a tumor." Once I heard "tumor," I was glad; maybe they could finally take away the massive pain in my head.

Surgery

I got admitted immediately. The neurosurgeon told my parents, "It's your decision. If we do surgery, she might die. She may never walk again or lose her eyesight or speech. But if she does not get surgery, she will die."

The day of the surgery, I said goodbye to my mom and dad. They kissed me, trying not to cry. The craniotomy took around seven hours. I did not wake up from the surgery all day or the following day. I got a fever. My heart rate was low and the ventilator was breathing for me. Doctors did not know why I was not waking up and ordered an MRI. What they saw was a small piece of tumor. The doctors said they needed to get that piece out. Four days later, I had a second surgery. I developed hydrocephalus and required a third surgery and a shunt to help relieve the fluid building up in my brain. After that, I started to re-learn how to walk, talk, eat.

Treatment

Doctors put me into a machine to get a blast of radiation to kill the bad cells. The radiation treatment felt like burning from the inside. I lost weight and lost my hair and eyelashes. I got so sick I could not eat. I also got weekly shots of chemotherapy. Finally, in August 2006, my treatment was done.

I Believe in Miracles

I owe my life to God and the great doctors and research done at Childrens Hospital Los Angeles. I have been able to go back to school and participate in radiothons, dance marathons and 5ks. My team name is California Edna and I love to raise money for the hospital and other organizations by sharing my story. One of my dreams is to write a book about my experience.

On March 5, 2010, I will be five years in remission. That is considered cured.

Ashlee Polarek, age 16

I recently went to a camp where I had to climb a rock wall, but I'm extremely afraid of heights. In the end, rock climbing was nothing to be afraid of.

Rock Wall

I giggle and laugh
but is it a mask?
Sometimes I don't know.

A fear of heights –
it takes all my might
to climb up this rock wall
we call life.

I look down below,
the people are so small.
I think of good memories,
I can't forget them all.

My arms start to shake
but I want to go farther –
hand over hand,
higher and higher.

Cheers from below.
I hit the red buzzer,
I'm not in this alone,
I can go farther.

I have always found reading my work aloud to be helpful. Words sound different out loud.

Food

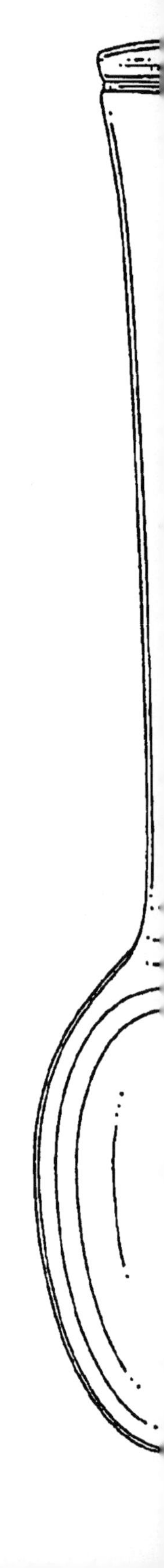

Something Crinkling and Sweet

Never write on an empty stomach.

Majah Carberry, age 15

I wrote this at the first WriteGirl event of the season. We were to choose a candy and describe it. The flow of memories it triggered was very surprising.

Life Saver

Like a bird's eye
An armada
Watching music
Hold the note longer
Smooth like ice
Glaciers of plastic and fresh pencils
The scratching determination and restlessness
Of something crinkling and sweet
That colors outside the lines
It's not timed but you wonder
How much longer
The musty library smell
Held off by mint green dragon breath
That courses, invades
You want more,
How much will you give?
Hold it close
Because it will disappear
By the next stop sign

Katherine Thompson, mentor

I love chocolate chip cookies, and I love poetry – this piece attempts to amalgamate those two loves in one short sonnet.

Using Your Mother's Recipe

for cookies, I am trying
to think as she thinks, intuiting
that intimate chemistry of sugar
and of spice, of white powders
commingling to rise and let the chocolate fill
the spaces left by their expansion. I have the measurements, but still
a mystery, elusive as alchemy,
remains: how has she
conjured those ambrosiac tastes time and again?
How has she managed, amid whatever human
failings she accrued, to master the creation of such sweetness? At times,
she must doubt that her life leaves any grace behind,
but I believe no better could be done
than giving to the world good cookies and good sons.

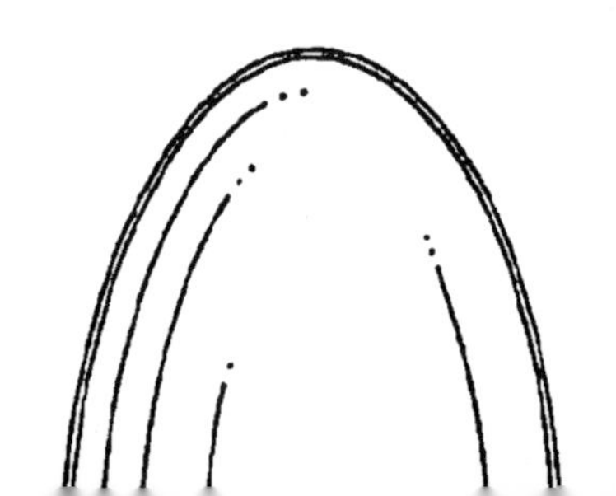

Elisa Mendoza, age 18

A Dull Knife

"A dull knife is a dangerous knife." My cooking teacher robotically repeats his well-worn phrase. His words seem to go in one ear and drift right out the other. I always liked the strenuous task of using a dull knife, using my whole body to cut into an apple, because it seemed as hard as a rock to such a lame knife. Tomatoes would always smash down and wet seeds would fly all over the counter. Ugh! What a mess!

When I won my Japanese cook's knife in a cooking competition, clarity came to me. Finally, I understood the robotic phrase I never seemed to comprehend before. This knife made cooking so much easier. Never had I cut through anything so quickly and smoothly. No force was needed. It cut through everything like butter. Now the words are ingrained in my mind: "A dull knife is a dangerous knife."

Rachel Torres, mentor

At our first meeting, my mentee and I wrote about what it felt like to be alive at that moment.

In the Fall

The air hits certain notes in the autumn. I don't know instruments so well, but I imagine bright violin octaves. The fresh air is crisp and chaps our lips. We hold hands and walk to the library to check out violin concertos on CD. We can listen to them while you watch football and I wrap gifts in butcher paper.

Indoors, the air is a hot, thick liquor. We tile slices of pink ham and spoonfuls of corn pudding on our plates. Someone's mother tells a long, funny story about New Orleans, punctuated by choice curse words, while I pick the wishbone off the second turkey, and rinse and carefully dry it. I set it up against the glass window over the sink. Outside, it's dusky and the neighbors' floodlights make the bougainvillea cast curly shadows on the side alley.

I've eaten quite a few of the fragrant bacon-wrapped dates already. They grab at my intestines when we start singing karaoke. I dance like a robot when Dan sings, "Mr. Roboto." We all feel bright and impossibly old when we realize it was over a decade ago that we first heard of Britney Spears. We are lazy on couches. Someone's mother brings out more pies.

When I think about what I'm thankful for, I think about us, and our friends, and our parents, and the library, and football, all the bacon-wrapped dates, playing fetch with a dachshund while you sing karaoke, and all our friends singing karaoke, my mom's turkey and your mom's pie, and what I'm really thankful for – I'm not sure what it is, but I feel it, I feel it in my whole heart when we breathe in, breathe out and the air is just so crisp.

Brianna Taylor, age 15, and Bonnie Barry LaMon, mentor

My mentor and I wrote separate haiku poems and then put them together. We always meet at Starbucks, so we used our location as a starting point.

Haiku at Starbucks

Starbucks is noisy
The coffee is very hot
We meet there often

My school is so big
I hate my history class
I love my math class

The human race
I run slow, then I go fast
When will I finish?

I love to get shoes
I give my old ones away
Then I get new kicks

I sleep in Friday
Do homework on Saturday
Sunday I see her

We talk and we write
Eat, drink, laugh and people stare
Then we write some more

Ciara Blackwell, age 15

I was in Starbucks with my mentor, and we were looking around the café for words that we could repeat in three poems.

Thoughtfully, Beautifully

1
It sparkled in the moonlight.
She tasted it, the rich delicious it.
It was there to hold, to dream
without compromise, made thoughtfully, beautifully
to last and to love.

2
It screamed
hollered.
Its voice
nasty with hurtful words flying
knocking me to the ground.
Trying to hold on to a dream without compromise,
made thoughtfully, beautifully
to last and to love.

3
In the faith that keeps us
from the brink of insanity,
I believe in warm cups of coffee
on hot California days.
It believed
in other things, boring things, and although it is gone
I still believe,
without compromise,
made thoughtfully, beautifully,
to last and to love.

Karen Toledo, age 17

At a WriteGirl Workshop, I wrapped my senses around this simple food product and this was my outcome.

Coffee Beans

Little beads of coffee in the mercy of the Christmas cup
Sitting in plain sight of the table
where the candles guard it with hollow lights
Tiny beads sing softly as I shake the cup
Such a sweet song is born from such violent motion
I thought you would be cold to the touch
but you're as warm as I am
Your tiny round bodies hug my finger
You're not as bitter as you taste
or as earthly as you smell
sweet little beads

Hadley Dion, age 15

It was Saturday, 11 AM, and I thought there was leftover pizza from the night before – but there wasn't.

Hunger

Hunger fills me and devours my soul
like a lion devouring the carcass of an animal.
He holds no sympathy for the animal he doesn't personally know.

The leftover pizza I thought I had is gone –
nothing but empty containers of Mexican rice
representing my stomach and my parent's vice.
They're hoarding the food all for themselves,
those gluttonous villains I live with.

I suffer and scrounge for something in the fridge –
nothing but rum raisin ice cream and chocolate,
condiments, soured milk, a half-empty can of peanuts.
I feel it's better not to binge.

If I had a car, I could drive to the grocery store
but I'm licenseless
in a city where the store is more than a block from my home.
Oh! Unwanted hunger, you consume me so,
right down to the very core of my soul.

Kiran Puri, mentor

This is from a longer blog post I published recently.

Goat Cheese Pakoras and Tandoori Bacon

My dad – an India-born, at-home-epicurean – continually fuses Indian spices together with my Minnesota-born mom's hardy, modestly seasoned dishes. I've gotten tastes, both delicious and disturbing, of Indian fusion for years. I'm surely qualified to call myself an authority, by today's standards anyway. And so begins my crusade to tackle Indian fusion cooking.

Spices are the crux. After dinner at my uncle's restaurant, the eclectic flavors of my meal imbue into my skin and the threads of my clothing, and waft toward me every time I push my hair out of my face for the next day-and-a-half. So I start with a manageable seven spices, all familiar to me: cumin, ginger, cardamom, paprika, turmeric, cloves. Then, I try to deconstruct the infamous "pinch of this" or "dash of that" system of subjective measurement, which usually leaves me with more floured fingertips and chutney-crusted bangs than delectable dishes.

In need of advice, I turn to an expert: my grandma. But each time I turn my back to the stove, she throws something in the pot with an age-defying deftness. "What did you just add?"

"Oh, nothing, *beta*. Just a bit of [insert Hindi word for a key ingredient here]." Then she shuffles off without bothering to translate.

The result is trial and error: *saag paneer* mini pizzas swallowed by cumin; curry cream cheese dip that only my girlfriend does not spit out; six batches of chai-spiced cookies that only start tasting good when they start tasting like pumpkin pie.

My cross-cultural, foodie mission will continue on. Next up: goat cheese *pakoras* and tandoori bacon. It's goat cheese and bacon. By today's standards, I can't go wrong.

Vanessa Cabrera, age 15

I wrote this piece during the WriteGirl Season Kickoff at the poetry table.

The Fortune of a Cookie

A fortune,
sweet and everlasting,
sparks a light that will guide us to our dreams.

As our conscience eats at our souls
like Ms. Pacman, eating all the little dots,
we wonder if this spark of light will ever fade.

Staying strong,
not letting our fears break us,
like a fortune cookie trying to resist the hands
of a hungry child from breaking it in two.

We'll make sure the light never dims
as it is the beacon to success.

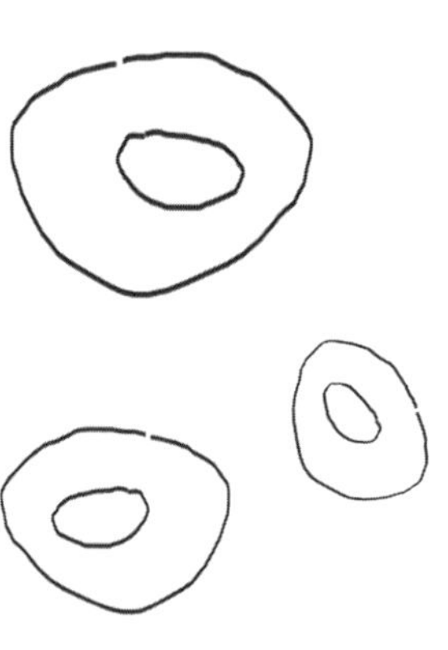

Don't be prescriptive about what goes in your notebook. Accept scrappiness.

Darkness / Light

light

Casting Shadows

Use the newspaper to inspire your craziest fiction pieces!

Samantha Nagle, age 14

This is about a family I know whose mother and daughter passed away in an accident.

A Miracle Lost

A single phone call makes the difference.
One moment there, the next,
gone.

Just like magic.
A sleight-of-hand trick?
Where is the smoke? The mirrors?

Miracles suddenly lost
in the rain,
in a blink.
Is it real? Is it true?

We hope, we pray it's just an illusion,
But reality sets in,
the feeling is lost,
numbness creeps over, and the stomach
is a twist.

We ask why it has happened.

Pamela Levy, mentor

Stasis

Early morning, Christmas
Oak tree bare, wires singing
Stretching against the wind
Trunk scarred by lightning
A huge black gash
Patched with pitch tar

Snow fell Christmas Eve
Crystal clean
Silent, impassable, tree-shadowed

One set of deer tracks
Sharply stamped in snow
Once around the oak tree
Trailing out of sight

Roses in stasis
Bagged against frost
Roots buried in wood chips
A funeral to Spring

Jalisa Francis, age 17

The Feeling of Summer

Hot, summery and oceany adventures.
My friends and I race to the beach,
a marathon that ends at the beautiful water.

We put our feet in and it feels like ice.
The sandy beach feels a little rocky, but warm.
We go looking for seashells to take as our prizes.

The feeling of sand at my feet,
the feeling of a cool summer breeze,
the touch of me and my friends jumping into the ocean.

The adventure of a lifetime, summer is just weeks away.
Summer and I are like chocolate and peanut butter,
and soon I will make my own adventure.

Lauren Sarazen, age 18

During the WriteGirl Poetry Workshop, we were asked to make a list of things we loved, and it inspired this piece.

Tonight

Waiting patiently for ten, eleven, twelve, and one to file past, the quiet hour between two and three AM is her time. Eventually, the soft footsteps in the hall fall silent, and Porter knows the house is asleep. She creeps up the stairs, ignoring the sharp creaks from her steps – now her parents won't wake up.

In the quiet hour between two and three, she paints watercolor pictures on the floor, sitting cross-legged on the faded pink carpet. She leans over the page with focused concentration, soothed by the rushing river of cars passing under her window. The room is lit by the bright white light from the tiny television – it only takes VHS – in the corner. It's playing *Sabrina* (1954), the sweet lavender strains of "Isn't It Romantic" mingling with the house's soft sighs.

In this dark, she is tense despite those fluid brushstrokes. Her insides twist, easing into that confusing feeling somewhere between the relaxation of sleep and the tight pull of muscle stretches. Like a fairytale, this place has 1920s charm. Open to the possibilities, unconcerned with perfection, she paints a dog with one eye and it is beautiful.

In the quiet hour between two and three, it's right, and the light from the television set runs screaming across the ceiling.

Lindsay Nelson, mentor

Shimoda

Rising from the sea
how those black ships must have looked
looming larger and larger, moving unafraid
toward an unwelcoming but curious shore

White sails against black masts,
black masts against white skies
figureheads with painted eyes
wooden breasts
pointing toward the unknown

Today's horizon shows only
a skiff or two, a distant oil tanker, a gray sky
merging with gray water
a space defined by absence

The black ships' ghosts
press forward onto this beach
into grains of sand between my fingers and toes
swallowing me in the dream of future ships
black, silver, creatures of all terrains
pressing me away from this beach
toward another unseen shore

I become fragments
one of a thousand ghost-pieces of other ships, other watchers
hundreds of years past
those who remember the wooden gods of a distant world
rising from the sea.

Isabella Anderson, age 14

I was inspired by the "Maximum Ride" series by James Patterson.

The Yin and the Yang

The store wasn't that big. It had a lot of stuff, though. I passed by old rusty guns (scary), creepy porcelain dolls (scarier) and cheesy worn-out romance novels (scariest). Then I saw a necklace – it didn't have any gems or anything sparkly like that. It was just a plain black leather cord with a charm on it.

"Whatcha looking at?" I nearly jumped three feet in the air. I turned my head to see a smirking, yet curious Fang looking back at me. I glared at him, then turned back to the necklace. Fang followed my gaze. He smiled a rare smile and said, "Yin and Yang. Do you know what it means?" I shook my head, no.

He looked over my shoulder and said, "The outer circle represents 'everything,' while the black and white shapes within the circle represent the interaction of two energies. The black is Yin, and it stands for all that is dark, mysterious and cold. The white is Yang, and stands for all the light, warm and bright things in life. As you can see, Yin is not completely black and Yang is not completely white," Fang said, referring to the little circles, "just like things in life are not completely black or white. In other words, they need each other to exist." He finished, sounding a bit wistful.

I turned to stare at him, shocked. "How do you know so much about it?" He just smiled at me (wow, he's been doing that a lot in the last few minutes. I wonder if antique stores have that effect on him?) and said, "Don't you think that the Yin and Yang make a good analogy about me and you?" I thought about that for a moment and realized he was right. "Yeah, I guess you're right..." I said thoughtfully. Yin was so obviously Fang, and I was Yang and we couldn't exist without each other. It was as simple as that.

Mary Ann Jurado, age 18

This piece is tells the story of a young woman's attempt to battle depression by sewing a dress out of moonbeams.

Moonbeam Dress

The sunset a glint of glass,
a frail grandmother clock whose hours throb,
the caress of the moon.

Before sorrow tips her over,
she locks herself in the tower
lies in the dust of evening song,
inhales the stars.

Wakeful dreaming in her heartbeat,
as the moon slices its beams
and from those she sews.

Her lips gently parted,
eyes glowing in twilight's psyche,
the threads hum a melancholy lullaby,
and a shivering wind grips her bare skin.

She swallows every sweet star
as she sews moon threads
into a pale glow.

Marietta Putignano-King, mentor

This was written at a mentoring session. My mentee, Majah, and I each described "longing" using all five senses, wrapping up with a metaphor.

Longing

Longing looks like an empty field of wheat
Dense and sparse at once
Swaying with each breath of wind
Longing smells like an olive branch
Reaching out for peace
Finding only desolation and chaos
Longing tastes of sweet melon
Embraced by warmth of the sun
But never quite ripe enough to pick
Longing sounds like the constant beckoning coo from a lone dove
In the hushed gold light before sunrise
Longing feels like dreams of love and promises
And gentle morning kisses
Waking to find you're alone
Longing is the ocean wave that wants nothing more than to be one with the shore
And with every ebb and flow
Is reminded that it will never be

Majah Carberry, age 15

Longing

Longing looks like an untold dream
A cloud chopped in half
Broken and wistful but never really there

Longing smells like an impossible craving
A sad shop of beautiful pastry posters
All closed down

Longing tastes like a desert mirage
Something fuzzy and far away, almost real
But who will ever know

Longing sounds like tears of confliction
Falling on dark pavement
The light you were following grows dimmer

Longing feels like a reaching hand
Pouring out of your heart
Making up stories to fill the emptiness

Longing is a bird without feet
Flying above the world
Thinking of the day she will finally land

Spencer Hyde, age 16

3 AM

Verse:
The waves of lonely minds,
crashing upon the pavement lines,
street lamps, silenced cars,
life behind mental bars.

I can't tell the stars
from the blinding city lights.
I can't let you go,
but neither option feels right.

Chorus:
I watch the clock and every minute passed, our distance grows,
Late at night my mind searches for what I'll never know.
I let myself fall into the dark abyss,
3 AM will comfort me and seal it with a kiss.

Look up at the sky for inspiration – you never know what you might see.

Cassandra Shima, age 13

The Stars

CHARACTERS:
Milo - a genius; questions the meaning of life
Jennifer - Milo's maid

SETTING: London, England - 1800s. Milo and Jennifer are in Milo's attic study and laboratory. Jennifer is cleaning. She whistles a merry tune while Milo gazes out his window at the moon and stars.

MILO
Jennifer?

JENNIFER
Yes sir?

MILO
Could you come here for a second?

Jennifer walks over to Milo. He's still gazing at the stars.

MILO
Jennifer, can I ask you something?

JENNIFER
Anything, sir.

MILO
Why is it that the moon seems so close
yet it's so far away?

JENNIFER
Well, I-I don't know sir. I guess that it all depends on where you are on the globe.

MILO
You see, young Jennifer...

He gets up from his window seat.

MILO (cont'd)
I've asked myself that question every time I look at the moon and the stars, but the stars have been giving me mixed answers.

JENNIFER
You've been talking to the stars, sir?

MILO
No, of course not. The stars have been talking to me. They've been asking me the meaning of life.

JENNIFER
I think you're going crazy.

MILO
Perhaps I am, young Jennifer...perhaps I am – but you're missing the point.

JENNIFER
Well then, what's the point?

Milo looks away from the window and turns to Jennifer.

MILO
The point is, what *is* life?

JENNIFER
But sir...that's a whole different question.

Spend some time writing in different places.

Shaze Williams, age 15

I wrote this at the WriteGirl Songwriting Workshop.

I Watch You Fall

I see you standing there
The wind is blowing your hair
You look so good tonight
I see the light, shining on you

Deep inside I think you tried
to speak to me with those dark green eyes
But you don't know me anymore

All of this and all of that
Don't tell me what's on your mind
I really don't care

See me now
I've changed my style
Took you off of my speed dial
Don't ever call me again
Don't ever call me

Nichelle Downs, age 13

Blind Living

It's a way of living –
it makes you cry, laugh and wiggle,
it's how you open up
to people.
It's what you express your feelings with,
what you feel inside,
anywhere,
anytime.
It's blind living.

"Let your copy cool." Leave it for a few days, or overnight, or at least an hour. When you return to it, things will jump out at you that need to be changed or fixed.

Lia Dun, age 17

This is the beginning of a myth my mentor encouraged me to write.

The Shadow Bottles

Fo and his wife, Anla, lived in a world where the sky spread above them like a collage of firefly wings. It was always bright, and there was not one room in their cottage where the light didn't stream through the windows. However, on the outskirts of their world without shadows, darkness lurked, and it would sometimes trickle in, contaminating the shining sky. Fo trapped these stray shadows in bottles and kept them locked in the basement of their cottage. He kept the key to the basement on top of the kitchen table and ordered Anla never to touch it.

But Anla was curious about what her husband kept so secret, so one day, while Fo was out capturing shadows, she took the key and went to the basement. The bottles of darkness were lined up in cases around the walls, casting shadows on the light. Anla rubbed her eyes, unsure as to why she couldn't see inside the bottles, but then realized that for some reason, light could not penetrate the bottles.

She opened a bottle, and the darkness glided out of the bottle and floated across the room. Fascinated, Anla released three more bottles of darkness, and she and the shadows danced around the room. The darkness covered her eyes, like a cool piece of cloth, soothing against the light. "But you have to go back," Anla told the darkness, "or else Fo will know I let you out."

Love

If You Want Your
Heart Back

Make a date with yourself: a tall, cold soda, your favorite music, and a blank page.

Ashley Symone Lee, age 17

At a WriteGirl workshop, we were prompted to rant and rave about things we love. This is an ode to all of the causeless rebels, independent misfits, underrated and erudite geeks of the world, and the people who love them.

Skinny Boys

I've never been too fond of them – boys with muscles. I can't get my arms around them. It seems as though I'm gripping an oversized, soul-exempt prototype. I don't like them at the beach, parading around, self-consumed in their "bro-mances" and dividends. I don't like them at parties, conceited and disparaging, expecting "some" from every woman in the room. I don't like them on dates, with their *you shouldn't eat that's* and their *I can't really get into Mozart's.*

I like suburban punks and Harvard-bound bibliophiles – the Maxwell Drummeys and the Ezra Koenigs and the David-Andrew Wallachs – the kinds of boys you'd find rummaging through 60s Brit-Rock vinyl at a secondhand store. I like them gaunt and bony, wearing skinny jeans that wrap loosely around their knees and reveal the extent to which they are knock-kneed. I like when they sport tattered Chuck Taylor sneakers on large, awkward feet that seem to have minds of their own. I like when their hair is carefully crafted, fluffy and conditioned, or even completely disheveled – black, ratty and threadlike, cascading past their noses and parting just barely to announce their insipid faces, fresh with peach fuzz. Their seemingly melon-sized eyes, keen with fidelity and uneasiness, peek out from behind clear-cut glass spectacles, and drive me barmy when they convene with mine. By some distorted, shallow standards, these boys are unattractive.

People will ask me how I can possibly love such a quiet boy, how I can trust someone who is so consumed by his skateboards and cerebral affairs. People who have to ask are painfully clueless. These boys are cultured, bilingual, multi-instrumental, unbiased, romantic, double-jointed, esoteric, weird, gawkish, nerdy, intellectual, loveable. I will always be fond of them – skinny boys.

Nicole Saati, age 17

I wrote this piece when everything seemed to be going wrong and I couldn't do anything about it.

All These Things

It sucks when the one guy
you used to want
doesn't realize what he had
until you are with someone else

When you feel like you have a best friend
but realize that people were right
about her

When you think you may know someone
and you look back
and realize you don't

When you and your best friend
don't go to the same school anymore
When you feel like you have been replaced
even though she says you haven't

When you wish you had already moved on
but they are still in your heart

When you feel like everything is going the right way
until you take a good look
and realize something is missing

When you come up with all these negative things
in life, but not the positive.

There is no bad writing, just work that might need (more) editing.

Cindy Collins, mentor

Some friends offered to set me up on a blind date, but before we went out, I realized we'd already been set up once before. It gave me an idea for a scene.

Blind Date, Part Two

INT. RESTAURANT - NIGHT

A man, PETER, and a woman, LINDA, are seated at a table in a restaurant. They are both in their mid-thirties and are enjoying each other's company. Peter is delivering the punchline to a joke.

PETER

And the guy says, "I don't even like broccoli!"

Linda laughs.

PETER

You have a great laugh. I can't believe you get my jokes. Nobody gets my jokes.

LINDA

Well, it's easy. You're funny.

PETER

Who would've thought that a blind date could go so well? I feel like I've been on a million of these things.

LINDA

Oh, me, too. I'm so over all the superficial small talk. Why don't you tell me something about yourself?

PETER

Like what?

LINDA

Well, how'd you get that scar on your chin?

PETER

The truth? I was chased by a bear.

Linda gives him a quizzical look.

PETER

Well, okay, it was a baby bear. Actually,
I tripped over it.

LINDA

(disappointed)
I don't believe this.

PETER

No, really, I was at this petting zoo, and –

LINDA

(looking at him more closely)
Did you used to have more hair?

Peter self-consciously runs his fingers through his thinning hair, achieving a bad comb-over.

PETER

Maybe. Why?

LINDA

I knew you looked familiar! You're the guy with the bear story.
(off his look)
We've already done this. We went to that place on the wharf.

Peter puts on his glasses and gives Linda a closer look.

PETER

Oh, right, the wharf. I got food poisoning because you made me eat those clams.
I almost died.

LINDA

I got a parking ticket.

PETER

Thanks for not visiting me in the hospital, by the way.

LINDA

Thanks for sticking me with the check.

PETER

Thanks for talking about your ex all night.

LINDA

Thanks for being an hour late.

PETER

(pauses; then —)
Look, that was years ago. How about we forget all of that and start over? Truce?

Linda smiles and holds out her glass to Peter. They clink glasses.

LINDA

Truce.

PETER

I mean, once you get to our age, you can't be picky.

The WAITER arrives.

WAITER

Have you decided what you're having?

LINDA

He'll have the clams.

Kyrsten Sprewell, age 17

You Were ...

You were my heart, broken into those little grains in an hour glass,
and when you were done pouring into the bottom barrel, you became
my alarm clock.

You woke me up with a tone, cliché and hackneyed, like
"Girl you know I love you," and your lies became
so loud that the sound vibrations not only beat on my
ear drums, but sang emo songs to my soul:
"If you want your heart back, don't ever trust me again."

I threw my alarm clock out so I could close my blinds and
sleep through the day, but you come back
when wooden mahogany floors creak for no reason
and unweathered windows introduce me to the cold draft of the night.

So, late morning walks to get my mind off of you,
only remind me of you.
I look both ways before crossing the street and remember -
you were the reason my parents taught me to look
both ways before crossing the street.

Molly Hennessy-Fiske, mentor

At the WriteGirl Poetry Workshop, I was inspired by the guest poets, who spoke about the use of sound and channeling emotions with simple language. "Poetry," one of them said, "is a clear expression of mixed feelings."

Coming Home

Key in lock
Clicks
Sticks
Could you have
Changed it
On me?
Changed
Your mind
About
Us
Me
Her
Key in lock
Turns
Gives
Tonight, you are
Mine
But
Tomorrow brings
Another
Locked door.

Brittany Marmo, age 17

In the Streets

In the streets,
all alone,
looking up.

Every night, this routine –
I see your face in the stars
gazing down.

I remember.
Do you?

That perfect kiss,
in the pouring rain,
and then you grabbed me
and said, "I Love You."

But now I'm gone
and you've finally realized
I was worth waiting for.

Michelle Armand, age 14

With You

They say all humans need love
But to give, you have to receive
You may treat others with respect
But what about us?
We were with you every step of the way
We try to help you but all you do is shrug
You keep saying, "I'm not getting any younger"
But if you don't stop, you won't get any older
Now take what I've said to heart

Beverly Dennis, mentor

At the WriteGirl Poetry Workshop, we were instructed to make a list of things that we love, then choose one, and use that as the subject of a poem. I wrote this for my husband, Larry.

This is Not a Lustful Poem

Beautiful black man,
excuse me if I seem lustful, that's not it, really.
I just love his head, his nose,
his arms, his legs, his lips,
and did I mention his lips?
I love his mind, his will, his swagger
The way he loves his mother, or doesn't...
I don't really care.
I love the scent of him, the sight of him,
his hands, massaging my back, my feet
and, no –
This is not a lustful poem,
This poem is about a beautiful black man
And every time I see him,
I just go, "Whew!"

Lizette Vargas, age 14

Love

A day
colorless and far away.
Why can't I see
that when the sun's out,
I'll be free
to fly,
to touch the sky,
but not to love.

Kathleen DiPerna, mentor

Despite the age difference, my mentee and I seem to be experiencing the same confusions and entanglements of love.

Surrender

She touches the little box in her pocket and smiles. It has been a long, slow-moving time since she last saw his face, heard his voice or touched his hand. It surprises her how quickly her senses can recall the pieces. The glint of gold in his eyes. The clean, soapy scent buried in the nape of his neck. The deep, low hum of his voice. His warm skin as rich and dark as cocoa. His mischievous, spirited laugh. The web they spun round and round until they didn't have enough room to breathe. Will he still look at her the same? She hopes yes. She hopes no.

Funny how she once had him memorized, like a melody that lingers long after the music has stopped. And now he's a stranger, unfamiliar and cloudy. Not hers. Her belly rumbles. She wonders how easy it would be for her to fall again. But before her heart has a chance to flutter, she comes back to her breath. The inhale. The exhale. The silence and surrender in between. She remembers how she's learned to trust herself. And how there's nothing that can take her away from her truth again. She pulls the orange, shiny box out of her pocket and places it on the table. It brings her back to the day they shared peach margaritas and laughed in the sun.

Don't think too hard.

Ashley Aguirre, age 18

Perfect Isn't Real

Richard: semi-neurotic, desires sincere love
Josh: Richard's brother, witty, fun, carefree, insightful

JOSH
Lights, camera, desperate!

RICHARD
I'm not desperate. I just have standards beyond the physical.

JOSH
Oooh, Mr. Sensitive. The women on this site are going to love that.

RICHARD
Can we just start recording? I need to submit this video to the matchmaker before midnight.

JOSH
Okay, in one, two, three!

RICHARD
Hello, my name is Richard Cooper, I'm 26 years-old majored in business at Columbia Uni...

JOSH
Cut! Are those note cards on your lap?

RICHARD
What? No!

JOSH

Then why is this coming out so rehearsed?
It's not a job interview. You sound like a robot.
He-llo. I-am bo-ring. Date me.

RICHARD

I want it to be perfect.

JOSH

Perfect isn't real! This is why you're single.
You give women these standards, standards
you can't even live up to without premeditating
every move you make! So stand up, shake out
all those answers you're practicing in your head
and tell me three things you hate, three you love,
why they should want you, what you want in
them, and reasons I know you're human.

RICHARD

My name is Richard. I'm 26. You can call me
Ricky for short. I hate vanity, liars, ignorance and
arrogance. I love sincerity, spontaneity... mainly
because I lack it. And I love playing the drums.
I want someone who is open to love, and lives
with passion, and that passion can be for anything
as long as it's there, and real. I'm human because
I'm afraid of the dark, I cried at the end of *The
Notebook*, which I bought for my mother for
Christmas. I go jogging and then drive to the
nearest doughnut shop afterward. I remember my
awkward teenage phase of high school and I know
there's no such thing as perfect.

Melissa Wong, mentor

I asked my mentee to cut out some interesting headlines, phrases and sentences from an old newspaper. We each chose one out of a bowl. I chose, "Are you next?"

"Are You Next?"

Are you next? In line for the cashier, I mean. You look like a nice person, so you can go ahead of me. You don't want to? Oh, I get it. You're a little freaked because the books in my basket are all about getting over a broken heart, starting your life over and how not to have a nervous breakdown. I assure you I'm completely stable...for now...at least at this very moment. Please don't back away. You seem like a fun, healthy guy who has an obvious affection for hair gel. I think that's great. I see you have some travel guides to Jamaica. Are you going on a fancy trip with a special person? Let me guess – she's a tall, successful blonde with large teeth. Am I right? Successful people have large teeth, you know. I read that somewhere...in aisle seven, I think. I don't mean to intrude, but do you really know this person well enough to take her all the way to the magical land of beautiful sandy beaches? What if she turns out to be a psychopath? A fugitive on the run? Or worse – a commitment-phobe with an unnatural relationship with pork hoagies? It has heartache written all over it. One day you're listening to steel drums in the misty moonlight and the next, you're stumbling around a Books-A-Lot covered in cat hair, buying up all the copies of *He's Just Not That Into You*. It's rough, Jamaica Guy. It's rough. Looks like the register is open. Step up. You're next.

Same Crush Monologue

Dear Holly,

Even though I know that you met James Franco at a movie premiere, I just wanted to say that I got dibs. Sure, he smiled at you, and gave you his autograph, and even maybe picked up the jacket you threw at him, but it doesn't mean a thing! For the record, I've liked him since *Spiderman* came out, and when we watched the movie together, you didn't say a thing. (But neither did I.) But whatever! Now after you've read this, you're probably thinking, "Oh no she di-n't." But I just wanted to say in advance that, "Oh yes I di-d." Maybe you should just back off, sister, because if I didn't, that would violate the "BFF Rules of Conduct, Rule Number 2." Ok, well nice chatting with you! Talk to you on AIM.

Your Friend,

Victoria

P.S. I think you only started liking him after I gave you that poster. So there.

Mya Justice, age 17

I wrote this at the WriteGirl Poetry Workshop.

A Clasping of Hands

With you is a wild sprint,
barefoot and vulnerable
through coco-colored soil,
warm with fresh nutrients,
absorbing the sun's touch.

Fingers brush against rough
bark of mossy green forest trees.
Trees that will hear, trees that will listen.

With you is an open fall
in a golden field with pastoral grass.

Quick winds bring scent of full-bodied flowers,
swarming sweet floral dreams around me.

With you is a clasping of hands.
It is here I will stay,
here I can sleep.

When you can't find out what to write just start laughing – it always brings up great ideas.

Carey Campbell, mentor

Tucson

We met across a counter and a sense of ease was immediate. Months passed and you wrote that you'd be here. I arrived late and you walked off the stage right into my arms. We slammed into a hug so strong, like a tree, and you whispered bashfully that you were sweaty, but I didn't care because you were here and we fit and I wanted more. But I left. I always left and you were searching for home.

Time passed again and we drove through the desert, with a back seat full of promise. I couldn't see you then, your halo a haze across my blistered, clouded eyes. You offered a respite from my truth, but the demons won out when the Greyhound drove me away. I left again, I always left and you had found your home.

Seven years pass...your name wanders from the speaker to my ear, building wistful sensations within me. The telephone tells of your tragedy as I listen to your soft sweet voice and sad words. I drive long and hard across the states of this land...and then there you were, tall, with skin the color of an Oklahoma road. I sat under a storm while tribal drums played, eating rain with a child not my own. A chain of hands linking strangers in a crowd caused a blast through my heart so wide that I still cannot wake without touching the hole in my soul. But again I left, I always left, this time to find my home.

DeAndria Milligan, age 16

My mentor and I did an exercise listing one-word answers for things that are frustrating in our lives.

Love Square

Roger or Enrique, Jacob or Jose?
It's a love square.
Ellos quieren hacer mi novios
y no se porque.
As if my life wasn't already hard enough.
Amor.
One word can change one's life.
Yikes.

I thought school was the only thing that was rough.
It's a love square.
Poor Jacob, so young and naïve –
he keeps asking questions.
Next, he'll ask me to be his wife.

Color

splash
Splash of Paint

Scream it; then write it.

Emma Holmes, age 16

I wrote this at the Poetry Workshop. Our prompt was to write about our favorite color – I was inspired by the color orange.

Orange

I am orange.
I am sunset illuminating a lover's kiss. A burst of fruit, and orange peel smiles.
I am an Indian summer, woven tapestries, and wedding bells.
I am sun-tanned children and bikinis at the beach.
A gypsy smile and long flowing skirts. A painted hippie van!
I am daisies and marigolds and tulips.
A splash of paint on a once-clean wall.
I am laughter, and the calm that follows after.
I am orange.

Jatori Cooper, age 15

I Am Orange

I am misunderstood
and nothing rhymes with me.
I have fun, in the rain
or in the sun.

Beautiful,
like a sunset radiates its color
across a cloud-filled sky.

The mind splashes with eager anticipation,
whether noticed in a room of ten, or seen
in a crowd of one million.

Inexperienced in love,
no empty heart...a crush.

Like a fire in the eyes
I am bright with life.
To put smiles on faces
or illuminate the room with laughter.

I am orange.

Marni Rader, mentor

I Am Purple

I am purple, dark and deep, ripe and hidden, luscious, sweet.
Mysterious, pulsing.
Vibrant plums and violets, fleshy seeded eggplant.
Blueberry stains on white tile.
Mixed berry juice with a tart attitude.

Keren Taylor, mentor

At the WriteGirl Poetry Workshop, we were asked to write a poem playing with a familiar phrase or proverb.

In Hand

The small green bird
flutters, stops, thrashes around,
tries to escape, rests,
then flutters again, less energetically,
its heart beating rapidly.
The frenetic batting of soft wings against my palms
frightens me also.
My heart races as I stand,
caging this weightless treasure.
Too light a hold and I will lose it,
too firm and I could damage
this tiny life.
No more than three steps away
in the twisted branches of the wisteria
I see them, heads cocked, watching, waiting, even beckoning,
each displaying a bright golden throat,
thin white stripe over the eye,
long dusky tail and slightly curved black beak,
far more rare than the warbler I hold
and within reach, at chest level.
Slowly, I step forward, inhale,
plunge my open hands toward the two yellow birds
nearly losing my balance into the dense vines.
When the rustling of branches and fluttering recedes,
I peer inside my cupped hands
at a single
purple
wisteria petal.

After you finish a draft, ask yourself specifically what you like and why. Seek clarity in your own talent.

Jane Gov, mentor

At the WriteGirl Fiction Workshop, award-winning author Sherri Smith asked us to continue this story: "She stalked into the room, flushed with anger, waving a red feather in front of her."

The Quill

She stalked into the room, flushed with anger, waving a red feather in front of her. "Look what I found," Cory said with a calm she didn't feel.

Aeric swiveled round in his seat and watched her drop the feather onto the desk. "Congratulations," he said, and turned back to his work. Cory ignored him, already ripping books off the shelf. "What are you doing?" he asked.

Still rummaging behind the bookshelf, Cory reached further back and found the book she was searching for.

"That," she pointed at the red feather, "is – *was* Risi's pen. I found it in the classroom where she usually sits. And this..." Cory opened the book and pulled out a wrinkled piece of parchment. It was unlined, with angry ink splotches across the surface. "This is the note left by the victim. Look at the quill tip." She thrust the letter in front of Aeric. He took it and picked up the red quill.

Cory watched him examine the pair. His expression gave nothing away.

After a minute, he lifted his eyes to hers. "And you think this proves what?"

"You know exactly what this proves." She tried not to yell. He *had* to understand. She was running out of time.

Aeric ran his fingers through the quill. "You lied to me," he said quietly. He lifted his palm. There was dirt in his fingers. "You didn't find this in the classroom. Where exactly did you find this?"

“I...” Cory tried to think of an excuse, but her mind wouldn’t work fast enough. There was a door slam below. She flinched.

“Cory,” Aeric stood up. “Please tell me you didn’t. What have you done?”

There was a loud knock at the door.

“I had to,” she whispered.

Sarah Huda, age 16

Red Feather

She stomped into the room, flushed with anger, waving a red feather in front of her. She was mad for multiple reasons. Her poster, the one advertising her Red Canary fundraiser, was destroyed. The one who did it? Her boyfriend. She stood there when it happened, watched him cackle with his friends as he pulled out his lighter and flicked it open. The breeze pushed that one feather to the floor. She ran to grab it, but it was too late. She got up from the floor. The poster was in flames. Every last feather was burnt to a crisp. He high-fived his friends and walked away, never acknowledging her existence. No tears fell from her eyes, but blood rushed to her face in anger. Was her cause stupid? No. Was her choice of a boyfriend stupid? Yes.

Lying on her bed, she tossed her phone back and forth between her hands. "Should I call him?" she asked herself. She finally realized he was no longer worth her time and began to dial. "Babe!" her boyfriend, Gabe, called out. He was outside her window, with dirty Chucks and ripped, smelly jeans. In his hands, he held a pile of rocks and although she had already opened her window, he continued to throw them one by one. She twirled the red feather as she leaned out the window, dodging his rocks.

"We're done, Gabe!" she screamed out the window. "Done, caput. Enjoy your life, Gabe, because I surely will enjoy mine now that you're out of it." She tossed out the red feather and closed the window as it floated in the breeze.

Jody Rosen-Knower, mentor

Coco

She stalked into the room, flushed with anger, waving a red feather in front of her. "Have you been tormenting Coco again?" she snarled at Nina, still brandishing the feather.

Coco was the headmistress's pet cardinal, and she protected that bird as if it were her baby. Maybe because she didn't have a baby of her own. She was so mean it was hard to imagine anyone wanting to have children with her. And so fierce that poor Coco must have been bullied into that birdcage, who ever heard of a pet cardinal, anyway? Parrots and cockatiels, sure, but cardinals were in another category - you only ever saw them outside.

Poor Nina did not speak. She hadn't touched Coco, but she knew better than to rise to her own defense. The headmistress was not easily dissuaded from her conclusions, no matter how hastily they'd been reached. Tiny atoms of anger flew toward Nina, catapulted from the headmistress's pores by the force of her fiery words.

Tiffany Tsou, age 14

One Feather

She stalked into the room, flushed with anger, waving a red feather in front of her. "What is this?! This is what I get for my birthday?! A feather?!" the girl shouted. She had found the feather on the table with a sheet of paper that read, "Happy Birthday!"

"Well, does this mean something? I have no idea what it's for!" the girl shrieked. She was so angry, her face flushed with the exact same shade of red as the feather. She went hysterical. She was yelling and her yells started to sound like screeches. She waved her arms around and they started to sound like flaps. The girl screamed again. Then everything stopped. There wasn't a single noise. Where did the girl go? Where the girl stood, there was only a pile of clothes and a red bird.

Doodle first – then write a story about it.

Friendship

Because, together...

Photographers capture only a snippet of memory. Writers can make the whole story come to life.

Christina Anderson, age 17

I wrote this poem because a friend and I are considering taking a break from our friendship.

Truth

They say there are two sides to every story.

So how do you think
this
came about?

Do you think
I
started it?

Or are you justifying what
you
did wrong?

Should you be angry? Even though you did
me
wrong?

Did you think your words would
really
help?

They say there are two sides to every story.

Rachel Fain, mentor

I've never liked loose ends.

Closure

About 100 years ago – okay, not that many, probably more like 20 – my friend Tom commented that he liked my silverware. No, that's not some strange euphemism: I had interesting flatware. I happened to hate this set. A lot. So I promised Tom he could have it when I replaced it.

At the time, I imagined I'd be outfitting my own place and getting spiffy new forks in the next few years. Tom would have his hand-me-downs before too long. How wrong I was.

Years went by…I moved several times and kitted up several apartments but never did get around to replacing those utensils. I added to the set from roommates' leavings, and I think some must have walked off with said roomies, too. Every once in a while, putting away the dishes or setting the table, I'd think of Tom. We'd lost touch long since.

Enter on the scene the magic of Facebook. Friends from forever ago reentered my life. You know how that goes…are you the so-and-so who did such-and-such? You catch up on the last few decades. Amazing, isn't it, how easily a life condenses to a few paragraphs and you never actually interact with them again? They're your "friends," and you get all warm inside when you read their status updates, but beyond that there's not much to say.

Tom and I are now FB friends. I still had that silverware, up until last week, when I replaced it with a whimsical pattern called Larch that looks like it was stolen off the set of *Beetlejuice*. I sent the old set to Tom. He didn't remember it, didn't remember my promise, but I sent it to him anyway. It feels good to close that loop, even though only I knew it was open. Tom and I were close once, and I feel a small loss for the friendship we once had. And I smile when I read his status updates.

Alejandra Campos, age 15

This poem is about how love is blind and can be found in the most unlikely places.

Farthest to the Nearest

Today you dropped a tear on the pavement.
I picked it up and put it in my pocket.
I felt the weight of it pulling me down.

Who are you crying for?

Today you dropped a piece of your heart on the pavement.
I picked it up and put it in my pocket.
I felt the stone hardness of it.

Who are you shielding yourself from?

Today we bumped into each other.
I smiled to myself as I felt the warmth of your soul.

Whoever it was that made you cry,
Whoever ripped your heart out,
Doesn't matter anymore.

Write as if you're writing to your best friend.

Mikayla Cowley, age 17

This is a friendship song.

Fishbowl

Verse:
She's going against the current
And he's swimming by her side
Finished with the water
They want to see the other tide

Bubbles will surround them
In this world without some air
How can they live so lightly
With this scaly cross to bear?

Chorus:
So dive under the waves
In the high tides and the low
They'll tilt you in one way but
You have to go with the flow

Everything won't stay the same
I'll be there when you call
You know you're done with this world
When you're swimming into walls

Allison Deegan, mentor

This is about the permanence of memory.

Digital Signal Processing

So many bursts
Electricity, love, heartbreak
All captured in synapse

But thoughts are physical
They have mass
They take up space

When I think of you
My head spins
I don't know where you are

Living in my memory
Weighing on my mind
Still falling from the sky

Vanished from one plane
Etched deep into another
Forever a circuit, in crystal

Imagine yourself in a different century.

Places

Take Me Back There

Foreign coins or a bus pass can be inspiration – keep things with writing on them.

Kate Johannesen, age 15

My friend lives on top of a hill with a breathtaking view, and I swear her house is magical. My emotions were raw, and my hand began to itch.

I'm Sitting Here

I'm sitting here on the floor at her house,
gazing out the window,
and all of Los Angeles expands infinitely below me.
I can see all.
It's quiet,
peaceful.
I'm eating dark chocolate.
A slow grin seeps over my serene face.
The walls around me may be white,
but the colors of the paintings bounce off.
I feel as if I have been embalmed in a sea of calm,
snowy,
milky liquid.
It's not cold anymore,
but not quite warm.
It's room temperature,
but I don't sense the room.
No,
I am sitting cross-legged on a powdered-sugar raincloud
perched atop her hill,
city sprawled below,
everything moving in slow motion.
This minute is frozen –
a permanent image,
a still life in time.

Tanja Laden, mentor

This poem was inspired by my experience renting an apartment for far less than market value, and my belief that money actually means nothing.

Queen of the Lo-Mods, sans rental insurance

Voice of masses
in the low-to-moderate
income class is
taking over your building
making herself a home.
In the shadow of the apocalypse,
Queen of the Lo-Mod kingdom rises;
proud chin of generations struck forth,
pushing through herds.
From the war-torn rubble of reportage
where print settles like dust on a war-torn landscape
and technology proves too stimulating,
an agent emerges;
gathering scraps of nearly-disposed odds
and ends;
making whatever she can from them.
Power outages, screwed off-Demand
windmills generating something.
Heart skips; not in a good way.
Feeling much older than her actual age.
Life is ongoing, not a see-saw, and more than anything, life is finite.
So did the unnamed preacher whisper in her dreams
while she was sleeping.

Alejandra Cardenas, age 17

I was inspired to write this piece after studying the French Revolution for the Academic Decathlon.

He Slept in Odd Places

I left my heart in Paris, with no one in particular, no one idea in mind. I left him waiting for my return on the *Porte d'Italie* platform, line 7, *Mairie d'Ivry*. Since then, he has managed to slip into valises, purses and the baskets under strollers and carriages. I can feel him falling in love over and over again, yet he is powerless without me. I find myself powerless to act upon the love I have found in *El Pueblo de Nuestra Señora la Reina de los Angeles del Río de Porciúncula*.

He finds himself exiting on *Charles de Gaulle – Étoile*, emerging above ground to a sunny day during a Parisian summer. I expect, upon my return, to find him abused and worn, left to roll around in the dirt paths of the *Jardin des Tuileries*.

It will be a bittersweet reunion, both unwilling to abandon the lives we have led since our parting, but accepting that life must go on, and we must live it together.

We will venture to the *Quartier Latin*, the entire time spent in silence, and then we will continue our way to the *Tour Eiffel*. Riding the elevator up, up and up, to the highest platform, looking down at the city we will realize:

It is impossible to find love in Paris.

Jia-Rui Chong Cook, mentor

I keep a travel blog, where I write postcard-sized entries from trips near and far. These were adapted from entries I wrote.

Postcards from Scotland

Edinburgh, EH1 2NG

At Edinburgh Castle, we lingered in the subterranean jail. This is where American prisoners captured by the British Navy during the Revolutionary War survived on skimpy rations of bread and beer. As they awaited their fate, they carved their names and the shapes of their ships into the wooden doors of their cells. They chiseled stamps out of mutton bones to manufacture counterfeit currency. I had never seen mention of these men in American history textbooks, but here was evidence of their presence and their restlessness.

Dornie, IV40 8DX

We reached the Highlands today, passing hills threaded with innumerable streams. Scotland has more water than it knows what to do with. It's as if Mother Nature left the faucet on. On the drive, I got to thinking about the symmetry of nature. The red-orange color of some grasses and ferns matched the hair on many Scots. The thick clouds obscuring the peaks of mountains resembled the wool of sheep grazing in the valleys. A multitude of stones salted the landscape in a careless pattern, so someone was bound to try arranging them. First, we saw lines of long stone walls, then, the impressive, severe Eilean Donan Castle.

Isle of Skye, IV55 8WY

After dinner at our guesthouse, we took a walk down to the jetty and marveled at solemn Loch Pooltiel and the purple islands in the distance. Though the sky is gray for the main part of the day here, the sun sets (and rises) with cinematic flair. One of the other couples in the guesthouse got engaged at the lighthouse nearby. I could see why. The scene was perfectly set – dramatic lighting, a strong wind, and silence all around.

Renae McCollum, age 16

I was on a tour of Black Colleges in Alabama. It was very cold and quiet on the bus, and I found a bit of inspiration.

Southern Breeze

I see the beauty of dead trees
A path of green, frozen on the grass along the road
The sun's warm bitter chill on my cheek

The forest, where buildings never rest
Even through the winter
I see your beauty –
The beauty of the southern breeze

Through fields of dirt
I see more than you
I finally see me –
Beauty finally unmasked
Southern breeze

Maureen Moore, mentor

This is an excerpt from a longer piece written in my travelogue after a visit to one of Morocco's bathhouses for women, called a "hamam."

My Steamy Moroccan Bath

We've made it to the famed Fes, Morocco. Donkeys, cigarettes, loud hollers and hordes of men cramp the narrow, winding corridors of the medieval medina, Fes' 1,200-year-old historic quarter. Natural light is scarce. Shoulders and elbows brush against my body. I suck in my chest and hunch my shoulders forward to avoid accidental contact with the passersby. The cold air pierces my face.

I make my way to the *hamam*. I've been dreaming of the hamam, longing for the hamam, and praying about the hamam. Visions of a hot, steamy spa waft around my head like the sweet steam ascending from the top of a hot chocolate. I need a retreat from the harsh winter weather, a moment for my mind to rest at ease, away from the constant company of males, and freezing temperatures.

Passing through a corridor, I enter a tiled lobby. The warmth immediately unwinds the breath I had held coiled so tight inside. The eggshell-colored tile brings a welcome reprieve from the soiled and weathered walls of the medieval medina outside.

Standing rather clueless, I notice the line-up of women on a bench, concluding their visit. Socks are being pulled over wrinkled toes, undergarments and layers of white thermals are pulled over children's heads by their mothers. Next to them, a cleaning lady sweeps orange peels and hairballs from the floor with her large broom. She greets me with a toothless yet sincere smile, and eagerly motions me to disrobe and initiate my visit.

I remove my headscarf and piece by piece, the many layers of clothing, save for my shoes and underwear. Looking down at my almost naked body, something beige catches my eye. Not even my pale skin could conceal the skin-colored money belt that still lay wrapped around my waist - its pockets full of my valued passport, plane ticket, credit card and cash. Vulnerable and silent, there I stood, half naked with my exposed money belt, for all of the guests of the hamam to see.

Alejandra Castillo, age 17

Boulevard of Broken Dreams

What in the world is he looking for
as he stands and sits and walks about the room?
Here, what do you want?
Here, you won't find it.
Here.

If only he knew...
I can see him better than he sees himself,
read him like a crystal book.

Order a sandwich
in your gray-colored coat,
come to life yet only for my eyes.
You're all invisible to each other,
an empty room full of strangers.
Study your enemies,
sip down that coffee,
neon lights build a view -
this will be my coffin.

I'm the observant bystander.
You are my TV,
a painting come to life,
a piece of canvas,
my Boulevard of Broken Dreams.

Lia Dun, age 17

This is part of a short story my mentor has been helping me with.

Home

I find myself braking at every intersection, even when the light is green, so that I can savor the art galleries and coffee shops housing hipsters wearing sunglasses too large for their faces – but it flits by. Soon, I have been dragged away from the vegan restaurants with wooden doors and overpriced vintage clothing stores of West Hollywood, into the green-tiled roofs of Chinatown and down the freeway. When I merge lanes, I glance over my shoulder to see downtown L.A. rising against the orange sky, and hope that maybe the freeway will curve around and take me back there. Then, I almost slam into the car next to me and have to stop turning around. Thirty minutes later, the Chinese shopping complexes of San Gabriel rise out of the ground like orange monsters with the characters for "luck" and "deal" painted on their sides.

I turn into a residential area. The houses are old-looking, like the houses you would find in some 1950s sitcom about suburbia, but with the picket fences painted yellow or green and some with SUVs in the driveways. My grandmother's house is the one with the sagging roof and peeling mustard paint. In the driveway sits my mother's dusty gray minivan, the same one she's had since I was born.

Here again. Back to the land of buildings that jut out of the ground like rotten teeth and people who jostle each other aside, screaming bright primary colors and twangy English – home.

Try not to cross out too much.

Reparata Mazzola, mentor

This is a true story!

Camping

"We can't get serious until I know you can camp," he said. I thought it was a joke, but here I am, standing in the middle of a forest, grappling with tent poles and folding chairs. The stream is gurgling or babbling or whatever water does in the wild. The trees are tall and shady and the ground, suitably cold. I watch my date make a blazing wood fire. Impressive, but I can make my gas logs roar with the touch of a button.

Darkness descends. Animal sounds rousing fear in my Brooklyn brain are interrupted by the aroma of steak and potatoes wafting toward me - a gourmet meal in the wild? The presentation is on plastic but the taste worthy of Wolfgang. It's time to sleep. A queen-sized air mattress promises that maybe I would. Rain falls. A million tiny drummers on canvas. The dim lamp affords enough light to read Henry Miller aloud. Romance is imminent until suddenly it's a monsoon. The mattress springs a leak, lowering us to the dirt. Mood gone, mud rising, we escape to a bed and breakfast. A bathroom, a brandy and a fluffy down bed. Wait a minute. No room service? Now I really am camping!

Raegan Henderson, age 15

My Place

I wake to the smell of dog
It's cold
I go into the kitchen
She's baking
It's warm in here and cold
Out there
I hear the crackle of the fire
Happiness surrounds me
The dog licks my face
I finally know peace
I finally know my place

Natalie Zimmerman, mentor

I wrote this at the WriteGirl Poetry Workshop, inspired by the things I love, one of which is autumn.

Autumn

I fall in love with fall.
The warm air smells like crisp leaves
And remnants of summer's ocean breeze.
Twigs fall lighter than air
From old branches with broken hearts.
There is a turning of an old leaf.
I fall in love with fall.

Paloma Elsesser, age 17

This is based on my summer volunteer job in New York.

My New York Life

The humid air hit my face like a blast from a hair dryer as I walked to the nearest F train station at Essex and Delancey. I got an iced coffee to help wake me up, but the energy of the city offered its own brand of caffeine. Many people filled the platform, and even at seven in the morning, the New York state of mind was in full swing. Headphones on, eyes straight ahead, some travelers peered impatiently down the dark tunnel attempting to spot a faint blue light indicating that a train was coming.

My early-morning subway encounters made me realize how New York really worked – people couldn't care less about you. As harsh as that sounds, I liked it. People minded their own business and didn't feel the need to smile falsely when eyes met, awkwardly. Everyone had their own agenda and someplace to go.

This morning, the platform was particularly crowded as I packed onto the train car. I learned to get off at the 81st stop because it was the National History Museum's block, and it became a routine to walk down 81st and watch the birds sitting on the grounds. The slower pace of the Upper West Side surprised me.

Half a block down from the corner stood a Jewish community center that was a little dingy. I took a deep breath and entered the building. I asked the front desk where Buddy Camp was and the man sitting there told me, "Go up the little flight of stairs." I thanked him nervously. When I reached the door, I took another deep breath and entered the activity room where I would spend the next two weeks of my New York life.

Claudia Melatini, mentor

Over the Rialto

No one could deny Venice was sinking. Like an aging screen siren, she swathed her visitors in stagnant love, left them drunk with her diminishing push and pull.

The woman pulled Marco's shirt, dragging him toward the bridge. "Walk me back to the hotel."

"I have to close the bar."

"At least show me the way." She craved a memory to take away like a scene in a snow globe.

"Over the bridge, right on Calle Stagnari," he said.

She stumbled up the first steps then turned and waved, conscious he was watching her. Water taxi engines sounded below, transporting passengers to their respective sestieri. Gangs of local teenagers gathered, exchanging inflammatory phrases over the myriad tourists. Many people were afraid to stand alone on the Rialto – she was afraid of forgetting it.

She reached the portico at the crest of the bridge. Carnevale masks dangled inside closing shops. And the view from either side: the Grand Canal; gondoliers and couples; water boats, if they felt like running that day. Rippling waves met the ochre sunset, the view of the evening's finale cut off by foundering villas. From this point on the bridge she couldn't see him anymore. She began her descent, over the bridge, away from San Polo, past the Santa Maria Della Fava and home.

Jamilah Mena, age 17

I was thinking back to warm humid evenings in the pueblos where chatting and play made up for no television.

El Pueblo

I can see the constellations in front of me –
stones of light that spray the darkness.
It's a sky so clear and benign in the town by the sea.

My feet carry me further into the pueblo where wind is bliss.
Townspeople laugh and drink on their porches, a nightly ritual.
And the wildlife join me on the walk, coyotes and all.

The town is united with nature, they share a mutual bond.
As I hear a wolf's howl, I do not fear it at all,
for the townsfolk and children let me feel that I belong.

A humid wind billows with acceptance.
I smile and look back at the constellations, close enough to touch;
they knew all along.

Keep a notebook with you at all times – short-term memories last only a few minutes.

Whimsy

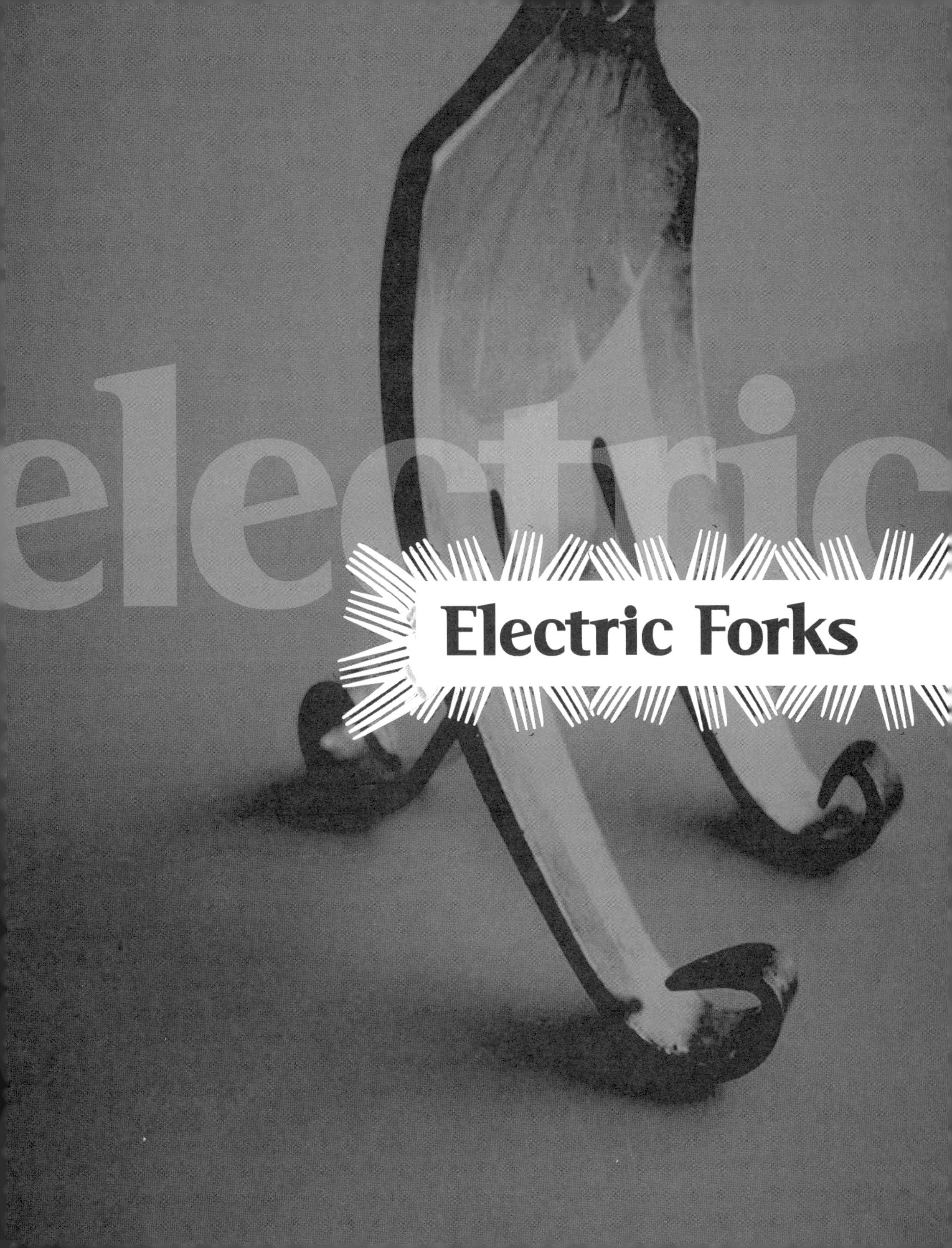
electric
Electric Forks

Porter Kelly, mentor

This is an abbreviated version of a sketch I wrote for a show at ACME Comedy Theatre. I played the part of the little girl.

Fearless Flyer

A LITTLE GIRL and her FATHER sit on a crowded plane across from a married couple.

JENNY
Daddy, is it true that most crashes
happen when the plane takes off?

Dad shifts in his seat, slightly embarrassed, aware of the other passengers.

DAD
Yes, I believe that is true.

JENNY
So when you crash, it's like...
(makes a loud, monotonous engine sound)
and then it's like...
(makes loud crashing sounds with big hand gestures)

DAD
(laughs awkwardly)
Okay, honey, keep the crashing noises down.

JENNY
(softer noises, then whispers loudly)
Why do I have to keep it down?

DAD
Because some people get nervous on airplanes.

JENNY

Oh. (light crashing noises)
Daddy, if we crash, can I put the cup on myself?
(mimes holding oxygen mask, breathing a la
Darth Vader)

DAD

(aware that others are uncomfortable)
Honey, we're not going to crash.

A HUSAND and WIFE sit across from them.

HUSBAND

Sir, my wife is already afraid to fly...

JENNY

Daddy, if we crash, do we get to use
parachutes like in the movies?

DAD

No, honey.

JENNY

Then how do we get down?

The Wife starts to hyperventilate and lets out a little whimper.

HUSBAND

Sir, PLEASE!

DAD

I'm so sorry. Jenny, honey, you have to stop
talking about this.

JENNY
I'm sorry, I just want to know in case we crash!

WIFE
(eyes closed, under her breath)
Oh dear god, oh my god, oh my god...

HUSBAND
Honey, put on your iPod!

WIFE
(losing it)
I DIDN'T BRING IT!

JENNY
Daddy, if we crash, will we land in the ocean? 'Cause I did a belly flop once off Grandma's diving board and it hurt real bad. Is it like that but worse?

Wife puts fingers in ears and sings "lalalalalalalala..."

HUSBAND
Sir, could you PLEASE control your daughter? My wife is going to have a nervous breakdown!

DAD
(to the couple)
I am SO very sorry. Jenny, you have to stop talking about crashing RIGHT NOW. Not another peep!

JENNY
O-KAY, I'm SORRY!
(long beat)
Daddy?

DAD
(with warning in his voice)
Yes, Jenny?

JENNY
What's a nervous breakdown?

Print out your work in a different font to re-read it.

Barbara Stimson, mentor

I started this piece at the Alliteration Station, one of the opening writing exercises at the WriteGirl Poetry Workshop.

Swing Song

Sauntering over to stand in the sand by the sea, I see, in a sidelong glance, the silhouette of a sad schoolgirl swinging slowly in circles. The secret of her somber façade is soon solved when suddenly her sister, Susie, sends the swing soaring and a sweet smile signals her satisfaction.

Kate Johannesen, age 15

On my dad's birthday, my mom and I bought him the most extravagant chocolate cake we could find. He had his picture taken with it and did not cut a single slice, but instead put it right into the fridge. All that night I couldn't help but wonder, "Why doesn't he eat it?"

Dad's 50th

My dad is 50 years old today. He has a life behind him and a life ahead of him.

And a cake in front of him.

Yamuna Haroutunian, age 17

At a WriteGirl Workshop, my mentor and I found pieces of paper stuck in our journals – the disparate noun and verb "horses conspire." We expanded on the idea by creating a poem entirely of nonsensical similes.

like a parachute

his hair waved like a parachute
the parachute fluttered like pizza
the pizza tasted like a parade
the parade echoed like sugar
the sugar swam like the moon
the moon shouted like soup
the soup shrieked like dust
dust jumped like chocolate
the chocolate swayed like Beethoven
Beethoven Facebook-friended a roller derby team
the roller derby team hid inside a lullaby
the lullaby drove to the light
the light was loud as a beard
the beard shimmered like toothpaste
toothpaste danced with a dream
the dream jingled like rats
the rats flew like avocadoes
the avocadoes flamed like columns
the columns were insane
insane
insane
the columns were the same

Rachel Wimberly, mentor

At the WriteGirl Poetry Workshop, one of the guest poets suggested picking a common phrase and then turning it on its head.

Glass Houses

People who live in glass houses attract voyeurs,
should have good interior design,
sometimes kill birds,
are exhibitionists,
often have faded furniture,
shouldn't have stone gardens,
do a lot of window cleaning,
always see you coming.

Never eat pistachios with soda.

Dog Death Reported in Santa Fe

Foul play is suspected in the death of Bill Cornell's dog, Cosmo, a 12 year-old mutt and alleged junk food junkie who was found dead yesterday of apparent suffocation from a potato chip bag.

"I'd made a sandwich and was looking for the bag of chips," said Mr. Cornell, still visibly shaken from his grisly find. "Cosmo liked salty food. He loved chips; couldn't stay away from them."

I hand him a tissue. "Take your time."

"He was on the bedroom floor, lying on his side at the foot of the bed like always, only...only his head was completely enclosed in the potato chip bag!"

"What a shock," I say, and pat his hand. "Do you think someone placed the bag over Cosmo's head?"

"We just don't know. His barking bothered our neighbor and she threatened to get rid of him. Cosmo had stolen chips before, but he usually ate them all and most of the bag, but this time the bag was half-full of chips."

"Let me get this straight. Cosmo was lying on his side in his usual spot, just as if he were napping, except for the potato chip bag on his head half-filled with chips?"

Mr. Cornell nodded and bit down on his knuckle.

"Any chance he could have died of natural causes? Heart failure? Allergic reaction to potato chip dust?"

Mr. Cornell shook his head. "We buried him under the peach tree. He'd started the hole last summer. We'd fill it in and he'd start the excavation all over again. It was as if he knew."

"What happened to the potato chip bag?" I ask.

"It's with him," Mr. Cornell said.

"Still on his head?"

"We thought he'd want it that way."

Think of what thing, or person you dislike the most, and write about them as if you love them.

Elda Pineda, mentor

At the WriteGirl Fiction Workshop, there was a Kitchen Station where we were asked to recall our childhood kitchens. There weren't any children my age in my neighborhood when I was growing up and I imagined what it would be like to fall in love with the boy next door.

Flying Robot (An excerpt)

From the window in the kitchen of 5008 Starling Street she could see into the neighbor's family room. He liked to watch Johnny Sokko and His Flying Robot early on Saturday mornings while he ate his Kix, still in his pajamas, hair smashed from sleep. She liked the way he laughed. He was 10, too.

Friday evenings (after finishing weekend homework, after being tucked in) she would turn on her desk lamp angled so the light spilled away from her bedroom door. Silently she'd get out a box filled with stolen tuna cans, empty Borax boxes, flotsam from the kitchen junk drawer. The smell of glue permeated the air, so she kept the windows open. Shivering, she assembled her model robots. As the sun rose she would affix a pen nib arm, or an unblinking button eye, and then lastly, she would insert a tightly rolled slip of paper into the robot's heart. Written in her best penmanship was one of many secrets.

Cradling the fragile figure against her erratic heartbeat, she'd creep across the lawn to 5010 Starling, barefoot and careful not to allow the dewy grass to soak hem of her nightgown. She placed the creature on the top step with a note, "To: Roger." Later, at her window behind the curtains, she waited for the moment he opened the door and laughed in delight at the discovery. A flutter of bird wings beat against her ribs as she pressed her fists to her lips to keep from laughing out loud.

She left a total of six robots that spring, before his family moved away. To Florida, she heard. She wonders still if he found her secrets and kept them as his own, if he knew how much it pleased her to know she could make someone happy.

Abby Anderson, mentor

This piece came from an exercise I did with my mentee at one of our weekly mentoring sessions. I gave us both the challenge of "updating" one of the classic fairy tales.

Sleeping Beauty (The Remake)

Sleeping Beauty had been asleep for 50 years straight when the Duke came to visit. She hadn't stirred from her bed, opened an eye, or even rolled over in all that time. There was a vigilant watch over her at first, but after 50 years, people had pretty much lost interest. Those loyal subjects who remembered the young princess when she was awake were retired now - and had moved to warmer kingdoms.

So when the Duke arrived, the King paid him no mind. He'd seen the best doctors come and go - to no avail. The Duke called himself a "naturopath," except that no one in the King's court was exactly certain what that meant.

He offended the palace housekeeper right off the bat with his pesky questions - How often were the sheets changed? Who did the dusting? How thorough was the vacuuming?

"Well, no one vacuums, of course. That would *disturb* the princess."

"She hasn't woken up in 50 years," said the Duke. "I hardly think the sound of the vacuum would do it."

The housekeeper went off in a huff, so the Duke did most of the work himself - opening windows, removing the flowers, dusting, changing the sheets and, yes, even vacuuming. The Duke rallied the grooms from the royal stables and got them to carry the bed - with Beauty in it! - straight outside.

Finally, he placed some "homeopathic drops" under Beauty's tongue. (No one knew what that meant either, but later they would speak of it as "magic".) Gossip flew around the palace, but lo and behold, an hour later, "Sleeping" Beauty woke up - 50 years, 8 months, and 12 days after she feel asleep.

The kingdom rejoiced. The housekeeper fumed. The King gave thanks.

"Simple," said the Duke, "allergies and chronic fatigue."

Jessica Alexis Frierson, age 17

My mentor, Abby, and I did an exercise where we picked a random fortune cookie fortune and wrote based on that. Mine read: "Success will come to your plans today."

Genius

INT. BOARDROOM – MORNING

The CEO of the company paces back and forth at the head of the boardroom table. About 10 BOARD MEMBERS sit around the long table.

CEO

Success will come to our plans today, boys! This is the day our company launches its biggest project yet! This will be a new sensation that's sweeping the nation! American life and society won't be the same ever again! We are going to change the world!

A MEEK MAN, a newcomer, raises his hand. The CEO looks annoyed.

CEO

What? Uh...

The CEO snaps his fingers, searching for a name.

CEO

What's your name, son?

JOHNSON

I-it's James Johnson, s-sir.

CEO

Well, what's your question – since you interrupted?

JOHNSON

Uh...umm....What are we selling?

The other board members snicker.

CEO

Ha! You hear that? The new member doesn't know what our world-changing product is! Ha!

The CEO composes himself and clears his throat.

CEO

We are selling electric forks.

Character

observant

Observant

Bystander

Don't be afraid to talk to your characters.

Carol Alexander, age 17

I wanted to write my first piece of 'personal and descriptive' writing, and ended up drawing on my "Pirates of the Caribbean" poster for inspiration. After the WriteGirl Poetry Workshop, I rewrote the poem.

To Jack

The way your dark mustache
covers the left side of your upper lip,
light reflecting an open berth of mystery.
The way you chase after black sails
hoping, waiting, wanting to bear
what was once yours, once again.

Your eyes confuse and excite.
Both irises golden brown,
lightly cover pupils of black,
onyx and snowstorms, hysteria and severity.

Those sails you'll chase forever
until forever is evermore and never again.

The left side of your Cara is as open
as the shadows on your right.
Your cheeks, covered in light,
seasoned in red; lightly sprayed with
a tantalizingly gentle golden hue.

Looked at yet never seen.
Dazzling, alert,
lying in wait for
worn wooden decks, shapely sterns;
and the Captain's wheel.
Always yearning for Black Sails.
Living in dark waters longing for their own sails.

Mister Sparrow

Laura L. Mays Hoopes, mentor

I wrote this in a session with my mentee, Victoria. Randomly, I was assigned to write about a lively old man, Christmas, a pool, and an electricity failure.

John, Floating

John went down the street for breakfast. They had cinnamon buns for Christmas, but he had his customary toast and tea with one poached egg. Next, he walked through the park, throwing breadcrumbs to the iridescent pigeons.

At home, he collected his swimsuit and towel and started off to the municipal pool. It opened at 9:30 but the gate was locked. *It's Christmas Day,* he thought. As he stood with his hand on the gate, a gray-haired woman shuffled out and unlocked it. He changed and left a basket of his street clothes with the old woman, who gave him a numbered safety pin to match the space for the basket.

The pool was dark blue and the ceiling, light blue with tiny lights like distant stars. There was one porthole-shaped window at each end of the room. John swam laps, trying to be one with the water. He imagined his molecules dissolving into the pool. John felt privileged; usually there were 10 or 12 other swimmers. *Christmas present for me, quiet, empty pool.*

As he began the next lap, the lights went out. The portholes glowed. John heard a garbled announcement; he thought it meant he should leave, but he did not. He swam to the middle of the pool and lay on his back. He hung in the water with no effort. "This is what being dead must feel like," he thought.

When he swam to the side and climbed out, no one was there to give him clothes, but he got them himself and left the key. He dressed and went back to the café where he had eaten breakfast, ordered tea and wrapped his hands around the hot cup.

"Is anything the matter?" the waitress asked.

"No, I'm just glad to be alive," John said.

Write, even when you don't feel like it – especially when you don't feel like it.

Jala' Curtis, age 14

Matchmaker Extraordinaire

Character: Amy Chanize
Setting: Home/Office

AMY: On my first day of work, I ate 10 tic-tacs, spent an hour perfecting my poof and wore a brand new suit from TJ Maxx. I looked quite dashing if I do say so myself! That day, my first client came in at 3:30 PM. Her name was Anna. She was a rotund woman who compulsively tied her shoes every five minutes and liked to spray perfume under her armpits. She had three kids by three different men she met at work. She was lonely and her kids needed a "papi." In the most polite manner I could muster, I told her she smelled like a rotting smoothie and her obsessive shoelace tying was odd and likely a turnoff when it came to potential suitors. She flipped me the bird and walked out. I quit, discouraged, lonely, ready to leave humanity and became a reclusive Buddhist philosopher that sold my work in hopes of financial enlightenment.

Palm Open

The man was sitting with his legs crossed at the entrance to the drugstore. His hand was held forward and his palm was open, asking for something. His eyes were sad and his body uncomfortable and he was shamed to be seen by everyone who walked by. He was wearing a clean, nice suit and a black expensive briefcase lay neatly beside him.

As people approached him on their way to buy something they needed, their pace became faster as though they couldn't stop because their lives were too full and busy. But even in their hurriedness they still were taken aback by the well-dressed man asking them for something. As they passed by him, he tried to catch their glance, hoping that his eyes would get them to stop, even if only for a brief moment.

Finally, a young man with a blue messenger bag strung tightly across his body stopped and reached for his wallet. He took out an old dollar bill and, with a compassionate smile, reached down and handed it to the man.

The man, who was watching the young man's actions in anticipation, moved his hand away from the bill. "Thank you, but I have enough money," he said, genuinely.

The young man, confused and surprised, kept his hand with the dollar bill outstretched to the man. "I thought you were begging."

"I am," the man replied.

"Then why don't you take this dollar?" the young man pleaded with compassion. "I want to help you."

"Because I'm not begging for money," the man said, again holding his palm open to the young man. "I'm begging for love."

Maya Anderson, age 14

I Know Her

I know her so I know
that this is definitely not right.
Why is this woman smiling?
How much of a task it must be
to put on that mask.

I see a big smile and a beautiful face,
wonder if there's any space for the truth.
How many people will wear that mask
and carry to their graves
unspoken truth and framed lies.

Diana Rivera, mentor

This is part of a longer monologue from a show I wrote entitled "Boop!", a historically-inspired rendition of Betty Boop's politically tumultuous origins.

Boop!

Helen is on the telephone in her boudoir.

HELEN: It happened...in a flash. (A sudden spotlight shines on her.) I always knew I had to be an entertainer. There was nothing else I could do. I was a loud-mouthed cutie pie from the boroughs. I worked the vaudeville circuit, trekking all over Manhattan, and then poof! One night, my entire life changed. I went onstage at the Paramount Theater in Times Square and sang the *boop-boop-a-doop*. I just put it in at one of the rehearsals – a sort of interlude. It's hard to explain – It's like *vo-de-o-do*, Crosby's *boo-boo-boo*, and Durante's *cha-cha-cha*. Then all of a sudden, I was a sensation! Now everybody loves me...I'm everyone's cutie pie!

(She looks in the mirror)

They all want to smile at a pretty girl, and laugh, and get flushed...even embarrassed.

They all want to remember what it is to have a crush, to fall in love, to yearn...because then they begin to dream. It's the dreaming that puts a little bounce back into their step and makes them forget all the lousy letdowns of reality.

(She looks at herself up close in the mirror, takes out red lipstick and writes her autograph on it, visible to the audience.)

What They Don't Know

Josie: a quiet, shy 12 year-old girl with a great imagination. Observes others around her whom she has never interacted with and makes up their life stories.

SETTING: Josie's room at her house, looking at her reflection in the mirror and talking to herself.

JOSIE: They don't know me because I don't let them. I'm protected by a thick wall of one-way tinted glass. I can see them all, but they can't see me. No, I've never spoken a word to any of them, but I know them all. I know their souls. I know where they live, what they eat, what they dream about. I know what happened to their mothers. I know what kind of cars their fathers drive. I know how their dogs died. These things I know. But what do they know? Do they know why their sister cried last night on the phone at 10:00 PM? I do. Do they know how long their uncle waited for them to be picked up after the basketball game, and how angry he was after they didn't show up? I do. But really, I wonder, do they realize who they are?

Elaine Dutka, mentor

I was assigned to profile the nation's leading Asian-American playwright, whose first original play in a decade was about to premiere. This is an excerpt.

Yellow Face

David Henry Hwang became the first – and only – Asian-American playwright to reach Broadway when his 1988 Tony Award-winning *M. Butterfly* took off. An icon in the community, he was a longtime advocate of multiculturalism – the concept that the U.S. is not a melting pot but a salad bowl of individual groups whose viewpoints must be respected.

Yellow Face, Hwang's first original play in 10 years, reflects the distance he's traveled since then. A comedy of mistaken identity, it suggests that "race," traditionally considered a "biological" category, is subject to interpretation and change. As boundaries become more fluid, he argues, the perspective must be global. The topic is particularly timely in an era of racial profiling and heated immigration debate.

The son of upwardly mobile Asian immigrants, Hwang is an expert in racial confusion. The American Dream, not Asian tradition, dominated his San Gabriel household. No one spoke Chinese at home or celebrated the Chinese New Year. He was raised in the morally restrictive Evangelical Fundamentalist sect or, as he puts it, "Confucianism in Christian drag."

Founder of the Far East National Bank, his late father was a bookkeeper for East-West Players, where his mother was the pianist. She'd take him to productions, Hwang's first exposure to "the boards." As a teen, he became an intern, building sets and reupholstering chairs. In 1998, the group christened its new main stage the David Henry Hwang Theatre.

The gesture is a bit "over the top," the unassuming writer admits. But, at least, they didn't put up a bust of him, as his Dad had hoped.

Let your characters do what comes naturally to them. Don't turn them into puppets for your beliefs.

Kamryn Barker, age 15

I wrote this monologue about a female character who puts up a tough façade as a defense mechanism to hide who she really is.

Tough Girl

No one really knows me. I mean, you may think you know me, but you don't really know me. OK, so I've been locked up eight times. That doesn't mean I'm...well, I guess that does make me a bad person. I may beat up, rob, or snap at someone every day of the week, but I know how to love. I have a cat. Her name is Rhonda. I love her with all my heart. I have a photo collection of trees and flowers and every beautiful part of nature. My grandmother was a fortuneteller. I have her old cards. Every time I look at them, I think of how cool she was. But I gotta show people who's boss. Not to mess with me. You know. I hate being messed with! I remember the first time I robbed a store. I was only nine. It was a rush. I felt like I had power. I'll never forget that. I used the money for my mother's heart surgery. But I told everyone I kept it for myself, so I wouldn't look stupid and sensitive. So, you may think you know me, but you don't.

Taylor Norris, age 17

I wrote this with my mentor, Dana. We always joke about how much I like to write about the first meet between a guy and a girl, so Dana encouraged me to write another "first meet" and this is what I came up with.

Glance

As I sat in the old, creaky, white plastic chair, I looked out onto the parking lot at the men in their tight green and blue shirts with black jeans, drying and vacuuming out the many varieties of cars. Bored with what I saw, I decided to open up my book and read. A few short minutes later, I heard a horrific sound and I looked up in disgust. The horrific sound came from a Toyota that sat on huge wheels. It was painted black with white flames. The engine turned off and the horrible sound came to an end. The door opened and out jumped a Bob Marley look-alike, except he had hazel eyes that sparkled in the sunlight. He handed the keys to the faithful washer and began walking my way. I quickly looked down at my book and tried to read intently again.

He walked past me and the faint smell of his Axe cologne lightly reached me. He entered the mini shop and exited five minutes later. I couldn't wait to see his face again. He sat one seat away from me and began reading a magazine that was sitting nearby as if waiting for his hands to make it his own. I stole a glance at him and his hazel eyes were intensely staring at me.

I smiled, he smiled and got up and stood in front of me. "Jeremiah," he said, extending his hand. "Leya," I responded as I took his hand into mine. Brown and hazel eyes met, and that's where the story begins.

Ali Prosch, mentor

I recently had a solo art exhibition that involved a nine-channel video installation. I wrote this from the perspective of the Travelers' Suite room at the Madonna Inn in San Louis Obispo, where the piece was filmed.

The Filming of Travelers' Suite

She enters with keen intent, hauling large suitcases and containers bulging with feathers, wigs and costumes. Cameras, lights and cords quickly follow behind as a troop of white t-shirts march in. Their eyes dilate with amusement and wonder, scanning Victorian beds, velvet couches and gilded chairs. They traipse all over my plush crimson carpeting. She directs the group back and forth, sitting here, lolling there. "Quiet, action, go!" Doors open and close. She wears several hats, oscillating between contemplation, frenzy and exhilaration. Her scenes assembled, magnifying the blemishes of my white rocky façade. Bell jars and crystal lenses examine my broken cherub arms. All the while, the fire roars.

Samantha Skelton, age 16

This piece was originally an exercise for the novel I'm currently writing, to help me access the main character's point of view on a normal day.

Sunday Morning

On this late Sunday morning, I stretch unconsciously and awake to the constant downpour of rain. A more modern *Pride and Prejudice* ambiance greets me. It's funny how the angriest of skies shadows down on my happiest of days. I open my eyes.

Beads of water are speckled on my window. The *drip drip drip* of rain plummets from the roof. A faint smile spreads across my face. A stream of light pierces through my window and onto my cream walls. Immediately, I know what the day ahead holds. I flip the covers to the other side and jump out of bed. From my bay window, I see the slick streets of Whiting Woods, Los Angeles, which reminds me I am no longer in the warmth of my blankets. I shiver and spring across my room towards the Venetian dressing screen where my Coco Chanel sweater hangs. In an attempt to keep the warmth in, I slide my right arm through the sleeve, then turn my head to look over the other side of my shoulder and slip my left arm in. My chin brushes the soft cashmere.

I glide by my desk and spin the old vintage globe. My subconscious hopes it stops on Europe, but that is not the case. I grab my journal and pen, and follow the aroma of coffee into the kitchen. The smell of German butter cake and coffee draws me into my morning ritual. I proceed into the great room. I cozy up into the Victorian camelback chaise, perched against the window that overlooks inspiration. I take a nice, long deep breath and open my journal — *Dear Journal, I think I'm falling in love.*

Jessica Alexis Frierson, age 17

I observed an employee in a liquor store while my mom and my cousin searched for the perfect summer wine. I wrote what I imagined her life might be like.

The Working Woman

She stands at about six feet tall, but slouches from long work shifts. She wears comfortable flats because she walks up and down the long aisles all day. Her hair is in an unpolished bob. It's easy maintenance in the morning. Her weary eyes and premature crow's feet are framed in a pair of small black glasses. She's tired of looking for specific liquors and tired of cocky minors. Her lips are thin and pursed. She doesn't feel like making suggestions or calling the cops again. She is wearing a simple black cardigan and tan slacks. She wants to be comfortable for as long as she can.

Her car is worn and black. It has to get her home after her long shifts. She visits the gas pump every other week. Her pierced ears listen to the cicadas in the dense woods. She listens to them for 20 minutes twice a day. Back and forth. Monday through Friday. She trades her flats for slippers and slumps in her worn chair. The voice of the talk show host lulls her to sleep until she wakes up later, hungry. She watches her frozen dinner spin around and around and around. She sets her black glasses on her nightstand and her head hits her threadbare pillow – reluctant to do it all again.

Guadalupe Mendoza, age 13

My friends and I each wrote a poem or a story that answered the question, "If you had an alter-ego, how would you describe that person?"

Sway

Although the light
is the opposite of her,
the darkness is no comparison
to her beauty
She is something more than us
I can feel it in my blood
from a pound of the heart
The beholder of power, knowledge
Shall she stand in my path or shall I stand in hers?
From her innocence
a smile upon me appears
She transcends our expectations
Creates vitality among us
For she has been marked
like this indefinable sensation
A feeling of
No, an untamed soul
wanting to be heard
Who are you?
Hear the wind touch earth and be heard

Yamuna Haroutunian, age 17

This is an excerpt from a longer piece I worked on with my mentor at a weekly session. We started with the nonsensical line "the clouds are indecent."

Martha Duvall

"The clouds are indecent," she says, glaring towards the sky. "They're far too gray." She crosses her legs and arms in one swift motion, not taking care to notice the alarmed glances from the mostly innocent bystanders. A few meters away, there is a small child gleefully splashing in puddles. She wants to punch him.

Martha Duvall is not having the best of days. It has been 32 years exactly since she'd been thrown screaming and crying into the world, yet no one has congratulated her for this incredible feat. When she had first woken up, she'd stepped into a pool of her dog's sick-up, slid three meters and landed on her back with a solid thump. She had to wash her hair in cold water, because the rest of the building had used up all the warm. Things started to look up when she made breakfast without burning her toast, but such luck was short-lived. She went to work – and she'd known for most of her life that work is terrible.

She leans back on her bench, twitching one foot impulsively, and considers going home and getting under the covers. Her lunch break has been over for 10 minutes. "May as well," she mutters to herself. Suddenly, there was a voice behind her.

"Would you like to buy some flowers, lady?"

She turns. A deathly pale, snot-nosed teenage boy was holding out a sad bouquet of red roses, waving the watery scent under he nose.

She narrows her eyes. "I'm not a corpse."

Pick a minor character from a favorite story, song or film and write from his/her point of view.

Magic & Myth

The Buzz of Tiny Wings

Always carry a pen!
And always show up!

Calia Anderson, age 15

This piece was based on a memory I wrote about at the WriteGirl Fiction Workshop. It started off as nonfiction about my first time catching fireflies, but then I decided to make it fiction.

Fireflies

Eden ran her hands across the smooth glass of the jar and smiled. Tonight was the night – she was finally going to do it. As she stepped off her back porch, she focused on a swarm of fireflies, their bright lights flickering in the darkness of the night sky. Poor bugs, they wouldn't know what hit them. With ninja-like stealth, Eden made her way across the cool damp lawn. Finally reaching the hovering orbs of light, she unscrewed the lid of the jar. This was it, the moment of truth. Eden quickly captured the nearest firefly inside the jar and slammed the lid down. Finally, she was victorious!

The young girl began to walk back towards the house when she noticed something odd. The other fireflies seemed to be following her. As Eden picked up speed, so did the fireflies. Soon, she found herself running as fast as she could toward the back porch, clutching the glowing jar in her hands. When she tried to open the door, she found it locked. Hearing the buzz of tiny wings becoming louder, Eden turned around to face her impending doom. Suddenly, the jar in her hands began to shake violently. Taking a closer look through the glass of the jar, Eden realized that her firefly wasn't a firefly at all. There, beating against the glass and gasping for breath was a little person. Without delay, Eden unscrewed the top of the jar and let the tiny man out of the jar. As soon as he was free from his glass prison, the little man flew up into the sky, taking the rest of his friends with him. Eden stared in shock at the shrinking swarm of little people. This had definitely been a weird night.

Marisela Toro, age 18

During a writing session at Starbucks, my mentor, Darby, asked me to use my wildest imagination and write something based around three words: Robot, Dinosaur, Alien.

Robot. Dinosaur. Alien.

Raymond never understood his seven-year-old's obsession with toy robots, but he figured it was better than her strange phase with dinosaurs and most recently, her sci-fi discovery of aliens in coloring books. To him, it seemed those things should occupy a boy's interests but he could tell little Gracie was not going to live up to her name. She was a wild child with more imagination than his own childhood and adolescent fantasies combined.

"They're my friends, Daddy. They peek out of my closet at night with their neon nightlights and a different board game every night."

"Uh-huh, sweetie. You don't say?" He disregarded his daughter's crazy stories. "Tell them to show you how not to cheat so openly in Scrabble," he'd joke.

That night, he thought he heard the faint creaking sound of the floor down the hall and Gracie's giggling. He leapt out of bed, catching a glimpse of 10:45 on the alarm clock and headed sleepily towards her room. He caught a hint of light underneath the door and placed a hand on the knob.

Slowly, he twisted the door open, making little to no sound. He couldn't believe what he saw – Gracie sitting on the wooden floor with stuffed animals sitting attentively beside her and three unfamiliar, life-sized creatures circled around a setup of Scrabble. Speechless, he witnessed a green studded Dinosaur, a bubbly-eyed Alien, and a silver tin Robot – moving, breathing, talking and laughing while teaching Gracie the fundamentals of Scrabble.

Eliminate your adverbs – use strong verbs whenever possible.

Rosa Palermo, age 16

This is an excerpt from a novel I'm writing entitled, "Elodea." Zarya and Nook are spirits from the land of Elodea who are helping Aric, a trespassing mortal, escape from the patrol spirits.

The Bridge

"Zarya, are you sure this is the best idea?"

"Nook," Zarya warned firmly.

"It's south a little ways," he replied in defeat.

It was early in the morning and the fog was still clouding the view of the cliff's edges. They walked a little farther until they were out of the forest. Once they came to the clearing, Nook left to carry out his part of the plan, leaving Zarya and Aric to prepare. "Start looking down where those rocks are. The entrance to the bridge should be hidden in them," Nook said as he left.

They found the bridge and got into place. As expected, there were three guards watching the entrance. Zarya made a bird call to tell Nook they were ready. The signal told Nook to alert the herd of elks he had been gathering. The elks started a stampede. Alarmed, the guards hurried to calm the herd before they ran off the cliff. Zarya and Aric started to walk over to the bridge and saw that there was one guard left.

"So much for being discrete," Zarya whispered. The guard seemed grumpy and lazy – an easy target. He was a fox named Bain. Zarya advanced to knock him out, but before she could, Aric stopped her. He threw a rock in the forest near the fox and this got Bain's attention.

"This way, we aren't seen," he explained. With the guard's focus averted, they proceeded out of hiding, stepping onto the fog-covered bridge. It was made out of old vines. Unsteady, it creaked with every step they took. They walked at an extremely slow pace to ensure the bridge didn't break.

They rested at sunset and made camp. To calm Aric's anticipation, Zarya finally agreed to answer his questions.

"Who are you?" he asked.

Melanie Ballesteros, age 14

After two and a half years, I'm about to finish writing a book – this is the prologue.

Someone's Calling

Prologue:
May 20, 1889

The old window was jammed; the wind came through and cold chills went down his spine. Fourteen-year-old Hal Noveroche wouldn't know where to look first if he didn't already know about the basement door, where she went in. He knew he couldn't have her, if only she weren't an angel...she belonged to God. Hal couldn't let her stay in the human world for long. Though he loved her, Euterpe would only think of him as a brother. He had never felt this way before. He would do anything just to keep it, if God wanted it to be. If not, let it be so, because God knows what is best and it would show in Hal's life, someday.

Falling down the stairs of the basement was one of the dumbest things he had ever done. Just to make sure the things in his knapsack were alright, Hal looked inside – his sketchbook was still intact, his Bible was safe, his clothes seemed unwrinkled. The new set of charcoal pencils weren't smashed, the money was safely kept, and her mask was in perfect condition. Everything was according to plan, though he was giving up his life just to find her. A few minutes later, Hal was right next to the door where he needed to go. Hal had known that the life he was living – great education, rich friends – was a good life for the late 1880s. But he didn't care. He swung the door open and pushed himself through to the bright light and gusty winds. That was the last time he was in his old life at all.

Meklit Gebre-Mariam, age 16

I suppose my inspiration for this piece would be too many spy films.

Alice Waller

My name is Alice Waller, and I need your help. I don't know who to trust. And the waiting – it's becoming almost unbearable. I just want to go home, but they're after me. I know they are. You'll help, right?

I've done something terribly wrong. I can't tell you exactly what, because then I would have to tell you the whole story. And now is neither the time nor the place. And besides implicating others – well, who wants to hear that whole boring story anyway? But you say you need to know. How else can you help me? I understand.

But I am sorry to inform you that there are limits to my flexibility, even in instances when such limits will pose as a disadvantage to me. However, I will do my best to assist you in any way I possibly can. You must understand that trust is something I have trouble fully grasping, especially considering these circumstances. But I do promise that from now on, I will tell you the truth or, in varying situations, tell you that I truthfully cannot tell you the truth.

So let's begin, shall we? For starters, my name isn't Alice Waller.

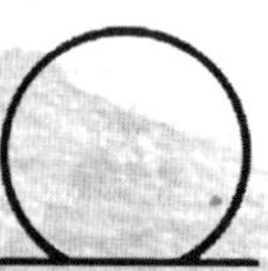

Leonor Cedano, age 18

This is an excerpt from a story I was creating about a girl named Isis. I was inspired to write her story when I was obsessed with the idea of having or being a twin.

The Land of Isis

Isis looked at Carmen. "I need to get this off my chest." Isis walked to the middle of the room and turned to the window.

"It all started when I was born. My village had a lack of technology, so giving birth to twins was not the best idea – not that my mother could help it. By the time she was finished delivering, her body gave up. After she died, my father went insane and killed himself on a hunt. My sister and I were treated like killers by all but our grandmother. My sister ran away, but I think they got her before she left the village. I have to admit that I loved my village, but the people were too closed-minded."

"I don't clearly remember the history of my mother and father but I do know some interesting things."

Isis went to the window and sat underneath it. "It's actually pretty romantic." Isis smirked. "At 15, my mother was in charge of looking for places to hunt and plant food. They say she had powers that could tell where the best fortune would come. Once she died, things changed and the village went into a depression."

"My mother met my father on a journey to a hunting ground. Some say that it was love at first sight and they were married a year later. My father was the best hunter and a fearless leader. He was a Chief and they followed his every move and command. My mother and father lived happily for five years and then they had us and they died," Isis sighed.

Sometimes finishing the story is only the beginning. Don't be afraid to create conclusions!

Jaclyn Cole, age 15

This piece is an excerpt from a longer story I wrote that uncovers events of mystery, suspense and misfortune.

The Suitcase

I had planned this when we had our meeting at the gym - two knocks, three knocks, two knocks, and a slide across the brown and peeling paint of the "Fido's Waffle House" back entrance. The door swung open and Mick and I stepped inside. A tall, gangly man nodded at us from within. His hair was dyed black and was stretched back around his head into a greasy knot at the nape of his neck. His face was covered by dull gray shadow, but I gathered that he was the Frankie we'd been indirectly communicating with for the past six weeks. We followed him down a narrow corridor into what appeared to be some type of staff lunchroom. When I entered, the first thing I noticed were the walls - beige, with Spaghetti-O's splattered against the chipping paint. There were three signs hanging across the back wall:

"All employees must wash their hands with soap and water before returning to work!"

"'Fido's Waffle House' - The best in town." This one had a small faded picture of a rooster standing atop a chocolate chip waffle, coated in thick maple syrup.

The last sign was framed in old, silver duct tape that was yellowed and peeling around the edges. "Food Critics claim #1 in the Country. Fido's Waffle House is 'The Place to Be!' - 1974" Given the date, I deduced that this was a restaurant that wasn't quite what it used to be.

"Take a seat." The tall man grunted. "The name's Frankie, I believe we've been in contact recently."

I nodded.

"So did you bring 'em?"

"Yeah," I replied. I knew that what we were about to do wasn't something they teach you in elementary school, but I usually wasn't a real nervous person, even in situations like this.

Objects

Fragile
& Precious

Write on anything but paper.

Danielle Flores, age 13

My Other Half

The secrets we shared are gold
Buried
Melted
Locked between us
Safe from everything
From everyone
But the two of us.
Now she's gone
Hidden
Torn from my side
My hands long for her
My eyes search
But she's far away
Past a place I can reach
In her own little heaven

She was fragile and precious
And I didn't realize
Without her, I starve
I hunger for everything we had

Without her, who can I share my secrets with?
My love?
My heartbreak?
My laughter?

Without her, how will I send my texts?
Or receive my calls?
My poor beloved pink-colored phone
Why did my parents take you away?
You have disappeared
But I will remember you.

Alexandria Rakes, age 17

This poem was inspired by a pair of amazing jeans that my mom and I didn't exactly see eye to eye about!

Allie's Ode

Waistband to hem
every inch covered in smiley faces
Hello's: messages from my friends
Doodles upon doodles
of yellows, oranges, and blues
Fidgety fingers make holes
pick, pick, pick, watch them grow
from Steve & Barry's to my soul
to school and back
up 11th street and down
stomping through SAC
my head high
happiness wrapped in denim
Oh yes, they stay with me
I really love those jeans

Mama's Ode

My God, that's my child
How visually repulsive
hideous holes and ashy knees
permanent marker stains
painted on her body
Mocking fabric
"Mira esta Niña"
Rebellious, "asserting" herself
My rocker child; that artsy child
She's a teenager
with her ridiculous friends
and way too much time on their hands!
Growing up way too fast
I really do hate those jeans

Kiarra Chambers, age 17

This poem is about my favorite pair of old sneakers.

Black Pearls

I call them My Black Pearls
They were with me on my first date with Milo,
and they were there when he broke my heart
that Sunday evening of sophomore year
My Vans were with me to walk off my stress when she left
Though these shoes are old now, I'll never give them away –
there are so many stories behind these shoes
My Vans match with every outfit
When I slip into my Black Pearls I feel invincible and even amazing
I feel that there is nothing to fear and that my dreams are near
My Vans are sturdy and sometimes dirty but even then
they are still beautiful
Take my money, have my car, lie to all my fans
Just please don't mess with my Vans

Christine Murphy Bevins, mentor

At the WriteGirl Nonfiction Workshop we wrote about our shoes.

Layers

My tan suede boots are worn down at the edges, but the center still holds. On the surface, these hip walkers are smooth, well-constructed, and fashion forward, all neatly tucked into skinny jeans. They're fun, flirty and youthful. But underneath, there is something hiding. The heels are worn down from too much digging in. Inside, the arches are in need of support. I should fix these boots, this mainstay in my life. I know how they feel: with a sore underbelly, it's hard to get anywhere. I should take them to be re-heeled and re-soled. I would see them strong and anew. Together, we could really go places.

When the time comes, we'll make a change, my boots and I. We'll waltz up to the counter and demand a new heel, a new surface that can take some distance. We'll explain that we have new worlds to discover, dreams to fulfill, a whole other life to live. We'll no longer sit in a corner allowing a broken sole to determine our worth. We'll get out there to the shantytowns and the shiny cities of our imagination. And we will be renewed.

List all the clothes in your closet, all the vegetables you like, all the times you missed curfew – anything. Then go back and add details.

Rebecca Garcera, age 13

Seashell

A tiny seashell
washed onto
my feet
with the sea foam.
I held it in the cup
of my hands.
Its edges had ridges
and many hard lines.
It was smooth
and polished inside.
As I held it
in my hands,
I breathed in
its lovely aroma.
How I love the sea!

Nicole Nitta, age 15

This subject gave me a chance to exercise my power of observation.

Pocket Pest

Life without cell phones
is hard to conceive.

The little square monster is a constant presence,
interrupting meetings and alienating friends.

In the middle of a conversation, it demands attention like an impatient child.
When you need it most, it decides to take a nap until it is fully recharged.

In the end, it's a love-hate relationship,
your lifeline and a pest.

Jada Obasi, age 17

This piece is about my cell phone, which has caused me many problems. I'm really attached to my phone and absolutely hate whenever it shuts off or when my bill gets cut off.

Dysfunctional

I've been neglecting you for a while because you have let me down too many times before. But without you, I'm stuck and unsure. No one has called. I only have time. Here I am once again with shopping on my mind. Should I move on and just leave you behind? We've bonded but that all fell apart when you left me with a broken heart. Now you're back and it's not the same. Everyone says I'm the one to blame. But I know it's not me. It was all you; you didn't do the things I wanted you to. And for that I'm letting you think about what you've done and everything we've overcome. Who knows? Maybe we'll fall back in love and build on the friendship we've made. RING! RING! *Hello?! – your bill has been paid!*

Jaclyn Cole, age 15

I wrote this piece at the WriteGirl Fiction Workshop, when we were asked to describe elements of our family and the house we live in.

What Lives in Shag Carpet

I grab hold of the rough tendrils of burnt orange canvas. I rip out the thick, matted fur that covers the beast born in the early 1970s. He doesn't growl, but I can feel this monster's ferocity as it spews dust and crumbs nestled deep within its fibrous mane from many years ago. The layers that sit caked within are like years. I see the golden glitter from when I was three and I dressed up as a fairy princess for Halloween. I see the thin streamers of black cat fur fluttering away from their hiding place of more than 13 years. And the dog's coarse hair begins to surface from many moons ago. Among the dust particles now spinning through the air, I notice the tiny granulated crumbs of those Mrs. Fields cookies I used to beg my mom to buy at the market. In my head, I can smell the sweet oatmeal and gooey raisins that used to belong to the few, crisped morsels. But still, I rip out the remainder of those memories to uncover a dull and stained wooden floor. It is not as nice as I thought it would be...removing those memories.

Growing Up

Things to be Done

If you are not surprised, the reader won't be surprised.

Katherine Bolton-Ford, age 15

I wrote this at the WriteGirl Poetry Workshop.

Fifteen

Fifteen is:
　　protons collide
　　chemicals react
　　exploring the taboo
Fifteen is:
　　puppy love paradise
　　predecessor of your first real heartbreak
　　the end of the world as you know it
Fifteen is:
　　finding refuge in Shakespeare
　　Romeo & Juliet
　　every love song written just for you
Fifteen is:
　　giving your heart and soul
　　to a boy
　　who would rather play Halo
Fifteen is:
　　learning from your past
　　mapping out your future
　　knowing where you want to go
　　clueless as to how to get there

Linda Folsom, mentor

I did a writing exercise with my mentee, Piers, where we started our poem with a stanza from an existing poem – I think using language from another poet can elevate your work.

Freshman Farewell

"Forsake me not when my wild hours come;
Grant me sleep nightly, grace soften my dreams;
achieve in me patience till the thing be done,
a careful view of my achievement come."
– John Berryman

Your dorm – a loaned bed, dresser, desk
Pieces of the child you were
Scattered amidst the borrowed
A stuffed blue bear, a blanket bearing purple giraffes,
A photo framed – you, swinging in Central Park, feet
dangling
in Mary Janes with lace-trimmed ankle socks.

I will not forsake you
Though you are too old to hold my hand,
Though your life will soon veer
Toward achievements yet unimagined.

This is your time:
Dreams are possible and there are things to be done.
Patience rewards me and softens my sadness.
I know you will return to embrace me when your

Wild hours are done.

Stephanie Peraza, age 15

I wrote this poem after I read the novel "Less Than Zero," by Bret Easton Ellis. It was inspired by the thought of growing older and not accomplishing anything in life, like the characters in the book. The title comes from a recurring line in the book, "Disappear Here."

Disappear Here

I drifted into the violet night,
escaped into the illuminated sky.
I dreamt of something I'm afraid of.
I saw myself in my adult life –
frail body, tired weary eyes, no longer inspired,
drained and living in the memory of youth
and of what I used to be.
Shaken breath, I woke up with tears crawling down my face.
My fear of growing older overcame my trembling body –
the thought of fading into a sea within a sea,
losing myself and ending in a frozen place, just like all the other
pale faces.
In this desperation, I wrote it all down.
I interrupted the universe for a split second before it reversed.
I didn't disappear.

Guadalupe Salgado, age 17

Tiny Feet in a Big World

I learned to live in my very own season where it bloomed
only once and snowed for its entirety.

I managed to plow my personal driveway with
my very own visits to the psychiatrist.

I even understood mind over matter, so I set out
to conquer my inability to reason with the world.

Only when I'm free
can I walk on my own two feet.

Piers Gunter, age 15

During the WriteGirl Poetry Workshop, I was having a hard time dealing with the average day of a teenage girl's life, so I wrote out everything that's happened to me in the last few years, and condensed it.

The Year

I grew up in January
Fell down in February
Scraped my knees in March
They healed over in April

I cried in May
Hung my head in June
Looked up in July
Saw the sky in August

I loved him in September
Kissed him in October
Lost him in November
And forgot him in December

The years of life
They've fallen to shards
Broken and useless memories
The ticking of seconds lost
And they refuse to come back

Kamaria Renee Holden, age 17

Chess Pieces

She looks around to see her pieces lined up for battle.
She takes the pawn and moves it forward.
She takes another pawn and moves it up two spaces,
being more strategic this time.
Then she takes the knight and, though a little hesitant, moves it forward.

Pretty soon all her pieces were moved in an unfamiliar way.
She looked at them for a minute.
They were her life, even though she was playing it
by herself.

She took the opposing side's king, previously untouched, and put it
in the middle of the board.
She flicked it and it slowly rolled to the other side, the way the sun rises
then sets.
It set upon the enemy's side.

She was done with this game. It was over.
She got up and walked away.

Read other writers, but don't compare your writing to theirs. You'll kill your own greatness.

Tanea Taylor, age 15

School Days

Wow, I'm so excited: one week off from school! I already made a plan.
I am going to sleep late and eat breakfast at noon.
Wear big fuzzy slippers on Monday.
Ugg slippers on Tuesday.
Toe socks on Wednesday.
Thursday and Friday I'll wear sneakers.
Saturday I will shop 'til I drop.
Wake up early Sunday and repeat Saturday.
Ride my bike, skate backwards and watch all the scary movies I can,
while eating cheesecake. I'll go dancing, singing and maybe even run on
my treadmill. But the thought of Monday coming so soon only makes me
wish there were no school.

Just Drive

Emotions bubbled critically in her mind, like a swirling volcano of molten lava ready to erupt at any second. *What was there to do?* she thought as she pulled out of the driveway, listening to the pitter patter of steps following behind. Not that anyone was actually following – it was all in her mind and she knew it. It was her former shell of a being, trailing behind, begging for a shot to come back. That old person didn't seem to matter anymore, for now it was all about the present tense, focus on the main issue at hand.

At this point in her struggle, she had given up on everything except figuring out what to do about this mystery boy who says he cared. Of course, she knew that he would eventually abandon her like all of the rest of them. He'd pretentiously say that he was a good guy, until he really got to know her. It always happened that way. No one would ever be there for her except herself, who had already betrayed her so many times. The fact that anyone would even try to approach her was too crazy for her to believe, so she had to escape to her father's car like she always did, and drive. In a way, it was her nepenthe.

After about an hour of frantically driving, hoping to hit a speed bump of understanding, it hit her. She decided she shouldn't care what others thought, and that it was all going to be OK, no matter what. Just then, it seemed as though she was attacked by who she used to be, and whatever the force was, it erratically jumped all over her, suffocating her, taking every gulp of oxygen she possessed. She soon realized that she was no match, and she gave up the fight and sighed in satisfied relief as she realized that her thoughts had sent her marching off the interstate freeway – she was finally free.

Linda Alonzo, age 16

Starting School

"Da-da da-da BAM!" I can feel the power of the music running in my veins.

"Demitra!! Stop that racket!!"

"Whatever, Mom!" Da-da da-da BAM!

This is one of those quiet suburban neighborhoods where the kids are straight out of a JC Penney catalog. The kids around here aren't like the ones down in South L.A. – here they're more "sophisticated" and whatnot. I've been living here for a month – but today I'm starting school.

"Demitra! Hurry up, you're going to be late for school and make me late for work!!"

"I'm coming! Don't get your panties in a bunch!"

"What did you say??!!!"

"Demitra, you're not really wearing that?" She stands there, her coffee in hand and a funny look on her face.

"Yes Mom, I am going to school like this – I always have and always will. Anyway, aren't you the one who tells me to be myself? So I am being myself."

I'm gonna win this round with my Mayhem shirt, short black skirt, and fishnets, partnered with my beloved Docs. I'm not here to commit social suicide – but I'm already antisocial, so what's there to lose?

"Sweetie. I know I tell you to be yourself, but look where we live now. Don't you want to make friends - not scare them away?"

"Does it look like I care?"

She sighs. "Fine. Where's your bag?"

"Oh, do you mean this bag?"

Mom had given me a new pink bag for school. Turns out, when I went to say bye to my old friends, she threw my favorite bag away. Since I was pissed off, I gave myself the honor of mutilating it...well, more like remodeling it.

"Demitra...you should know better."

"Mom, obviously I am a teenager and a very sarcastic one."

"Fine, 'Miss Sarcastic'. Let's go."

Whoop-Dee-DOO...Great, a new school.

Laura Lujan, age 14

I helped babysit my Aunt Yvette's children when her mother was very ill. They kept asking what I wanted in return, but I didn't want anything.

Letter for My Tia

I'm doing it because I want to, not because I was forced. I knew deep inside I wouldn't be complete if I didn't come here and help. I wouldn't sleep at night. It may not have been my idea (which sucks, because it was a really good idea). I gained from it. Gained some love. Gained some responsibility, peace of mind, improvement in myself.

Home is far away, but everything is fine. I know that compassion is the only thing that's keeping me up – that and the Oreo cookies I'm allowed to eat. I've never felt so happy, in my short life. So comfortable in a bed that's not mine. So overwhelmed with the desire to do something. Let me wash clothes? The dishes? Sweep the floor? Make the food? Feed the baby? Run around? Tell me how to help and I will.

Read the kind of books you want to write – then, read everything else.

Family

field
MARIANNE
JOHN
THOMAS
JAMES
SUZANNE
Force Field

Tiffany Tsou, age 14

I wrote this when I was reading "Anne Frank" in class – I felt that she and Margot are like my sister and I.

Half-Right

Older sisters are great,
if you're crazy.

Isn't it annoying
to have someone who always bothers you,
living over the same roof?

People usually think the younger sibling
is the weird and annoying one, the older sibling
calm and collected.

Those people would be half-right.

The younger sibling is also cool and fun,
the older sibling also strange
and unusual.

The older sibling is a goody-two-shoes girl.
The younger one is loud and disrespectful.
I'm the younger one in my family

and all those things apply.

Eva Joan Robles, age 14

I was inspired by my mentor and the people I love the most.

My Mother

A great heart, heavy as a brick of gold.
She's delightful and sensitive. Green,
O green her favorite color. Green eyes,
white skin, brown hair, a beautiful lady,
gentle as a feather, clean as her jewelry
when she polishes it.

My mother listens to me when I feel lonely
and abandoned. Helps me
with my homework, plays with my sister and me.
The way she dances reminds me of a graceful swan.
When I don't do my chores,
her mad face pierces me as if I did something
really wrong, but her voice remains soft and mild.
The perfect mother for us.

Jacqueline Jaffe, mentor

I started this in one of my mentoring sessions – trying to get inside the mind of someone different in age and circumstance than me – an 11-year-old girl.

Gypsy

Anna counted the steps up to her father's apartment – seventeen – just as she remembered. She loved the cool precision of numbers; they were never sketchy or vague. Numbers were something you could rely on.

The small apartment looked the same as ever – not much furniture besides the pine coffee table and the brown sofa that pulled out into a bed that Matthew, her older brother, would sleep on until he got his room back when Anna left at the end of the summer. When she was little, the tiny corner kitchen off the dining area reminded Anna of one of those Playskool kitchen sets that other kids got for Christmas.

She thought of it as her own play kitchen where she could stand on the wooden stool and mix magic potions over the sink from the likes of dishwashing soap, squeezed lemons and anything else she dug up from the fridge, even hot sauce. Once, she begged Matthew to taste it and he spit the goo back in the sink, screaming all the way to the bathroom until he brushed the taste out of his mouth.

After the three of them had devoured too many tacos for dinner, Anna cleared the dinner dishes from the table and placed them in the sink. Finally, she could reach the faucet without standing on the wooden stool, which made her long for the old days. When she heard voices rising from the other room, she turned off the water to listen.

"I said no. You're staying home tonight. Hand over the car keys."

"I don't have to listen to you," Matthew screamed at their father.

Anna had heard enough. She turned the faucet back on as she counted the small white tiles on the counter next to the sink: 155, including the extra row on the backsplash.

Create a writing schedule, and stick to it.

Ashley Contreras, age 13

My Family

My family is my heart.
They help me advance my dream of becoming a nurse.

My family is joyful dinners together around the table, laughing and having a great time.
They are my cheerleaders, helping me to do better, swim faster and think positively.

My family makes my world bright.
They have made me who I am, and every day I try to be better.

My family is the sun, and I am a sunflower
who never stops growing
as long as their light
shines upon me.

Teresa Rochester, mentor

This poem about my mom came to me came to me while I was standing at my kitchen counter one morning, making breakfast. Whenever I make bacon, I think of her. I've spent a number of sessions with my mentee, Isabel, revising this piece.

Predisposed

Mom talks to bacon,
chiding the fatty, hissing strips to fry faster.
The terra cotta frog on the neighbor's balcony is really a prince,
she insists.
I roll my eyes, but sneak peeks when I walk by.
The Frog King has stepped into his sauna,
whenever fog tumbles down the foothills, she says, solemn as clergy.
It's no wonder words ricochet like scattered marbles around my head
at all hours.
Fragments, sentences, paragraphs, stories,
my life's work, a genetic predisposition.

Start with a "day dump" – get everything about your day out on the page. Then start working.

Quran Shaheed, age 17

My cousin's confidence inspired me to write about him.

Cousin Chico

He is Atlas – he scales mountains and swims oceans.
Menacing and bold, a challenging edge to his voice,
he waits for fate to make its move
knowing he would not lose
but not quite sure of winning.
He forges ahead.

Laughing in the face of danger,
he tickles the belly of fright and smirks at shadows.
He makes rocks smile and trees quiver.
He is his own force field.

He is prepared for the worst.
He has mastered shock and awe.
He is macho and gallant, my protector above all.
He is my cousin Chico.

Evelyn Hammid, Ashaki Jackson, and Celine Malanum, mentors

This is for our beautiful friend, Natasha. It is a variation on the renga, a collaborative form of Japanese poetry with haikus.

Washing

Things began to fail.
We held our breath for peace – prayed
it would wash us new.

Things that you did for
Us – Father, Husband, Dreamer –
were slowly removed.

To live on our own,
guidance was slowly removed.
Now we must miss you.

We hold hands and trust
being held by words like your
small caesuraed heart.

Slowly, slowly we
weep our peace. Our wet faces
the inheritance.

We pray these heavy
things are slowly removed. Pray
for release. Pray us free.

You are now water –
amaranthine. Always you
washing over me.

Your fluid body
ripples outward. Prayers blooming
from our family's mouths.

Brittany Michelson, mentor

This is a poem written in the voice of Luna, the teenage protagonist in my young adult novel. She is talking about her friend Carly's family dynamic.

A Real Family

Carly has a real family
The kind with a mom, dad, and sister
A white house with green shutters
Two stories, two-car garage, white fence, neatly trimmed lawn
Even a dog in back to protect them from strangers
Though Woolsey wouldn't hurt a fly

Carly's family has dinner together with their own set places
Mr. P at the head, Mrs. P on the other end
And Carly with her sister in the middle
When I eat dinner with them
They pull an extra chair up for me
I feel like the fifth wheel on a double date

Carly says it's not all it's cracked up to be
That her family yells when no one's around
That her dad has a temper
That her mom cries a lot
That her sister stays out way past curfew
Even the dog sometimes whines for no reason

Sometimes I wish so bad for a sister
Someone to tell my secrets and my crushes to
Someone to share the lonely times with
Even if we fought I wouldn't care
I would give her the front seat
I wouldn't borrow her clothes without asking
I wouldn't drink the last of the milk just to make her mad

Nancy Lara, age 13

I wrote this while sitting in an odd-looking chair outside my house, looking at the rain.

Rain

I'm outside, staring at the sky,
with the rain pouring down as if the sky was crying,
tears fill my eyes.

Perfect tragedies are going on,
that can affect your own world.
It's hard to deal with it –
your dad not speaking to you,
almost the whole family against you...

What can I do?
Run away and never come back?
This unknown world makes me feel alone,
but when the rain splashes on me,

I feel and hear it whispering to me,
saying, "I'm always going to be with you,
You are never alone, I will remain in your
heart for eternity."

Kirsten Giles, mentor

This poem was inspired by a memorable childhood experience.

Pavlova

Madame Francesca's gnarled hands
hold my feet, study their shape.
She writes "Pavlova 3B" on paper
that is one side cut,
and one side torn.

The paper trembles in the air
between my mother and I
before it is slipped
between the pages of a book.
I am told to be patient.

On my birthday,
I wear my new slippers to bed
and dream that I am prettier
than my sister. I dream
that my footsteps land
like the whisper of falling leaves.

Lia Dun, age 17

These are three haikus based on the Chinese names of my grandmother, my mother and me.

Chinese Names

Sheets of glowing jade
shattered against granite slabs
never wanted calm

Lotus in the fog
blossomed between sidewalk cracks
spits acid raindrops

Named for harmony,
this river forgets to flow,
peters out instead.

Listen to your characters. Let them tell you the story.

Writing Experiments

Instant Inspiration

Writing Experiment: Radical Recipes

Take an emotion or concept and write a recipe using the structure and form you might find in a cookbook. Play with the list of ingredients, directions and any other warnings or recommendations to emphasize the feeling or idea you have chosen. Play with extremely large or miniscule quantities of items - take it to extremes.

Leslie Rodriguez, age 18

My mentor and I did an exercise from the WriteGirl Poetry Workshop handout that asked me to choose a subject and write about it as if it were a recipe.

Recipe for a Fight (Love Sprinkles Optional)

Ingredients:
3 cups of anger
1 gallon of shouting
2 liters hard-headedness
1 cell phone (for contact and yelling)
1-3 excuses for fighting

Step 1: Call, make an excuse that he doesn't understand. Scream until you can't anymore. Remember not to give him time to speak.

Step 2: Cry. Let him know you are crushed.

Step 3: Break it off. Hang up. (If bored, repeat steps 1-3.)

Step 4: Let simmer until he calls to apologize. (This usually takes 20-40 minutes.) Make it all lovely again.

DANGER: Overuse of this recipe could lead to a real breakup. Use with caution. Parental supervision advised.

Writing Experiment: Follow These Steps!

Instructions are all around us, from how to put a bookcase together to how to start your own blog. Think of an event, a day, a person, a phobia or a place, and write detailed instructions on how to do something related to that item. You could write instructions on how to plan it, survive it, end it, get over it, lose it or have fun with it. Be sure to include any exceptions, exclusions, side effects or special considerations.

Instructions for the Last Morning of Summer Vacation

Warning: This may not work, if (a) your mom signed you up for a last week of summer camp, or (b) you have annoying younger siblings, or (c) there are other circumstances I cannot be held responsible for.

1. As you emerge into wakefulness, do not open your eyes. Rejoice that you have the complete freedom to keep them closed for as long as you wish. Refrain from checking your clock.
2. Give in to the suspense and check your clock. Contemplate the idea that tomorrow, at this time, you will already be on the bus.
3. Further rejoice that no alarm is set for today. Close your eyes again.
4. Consider the idea that this is the last day of summer vacation and maybe you should not spend it in bed.
5. Quickly snuff this idea and snuggle deeper into blankets.

Note: At this point, if any annoying siblings happen to come checking to see if you are up, feign sleep.

6. Remember that you are halfway through a book.
7. Weigh the pros and cons of getting out of bed, even momentarily, to turn on the light.
8. Reluctantly leave your warm cocoon, but return in all possible haste, with book in hand, before your blankets lose their wonderful heat.
9. Snuggle back into your warm covers.

Note: If your covers have lost their warmth during the time it took you to turn on the light and retrieve your book, tuck covers around knees, feet, sides and head. Your warmth should be back soon.

10. Turn around so you are lying on your stomach and forearms.
11. With building anticipation, begin to read.
12. Continue to read until a parent, hunger, or the end of your book drives you from your refuge.

Writing Experiment: I am a...

Personify an object by giving it a voice. Pretend you are that object. See, feel and hear things from the perspective of that object. Experience life through its eyes and see where it takes you. Play with the genre - for example, you could write in the form of a poem, a scene or an essay.

Piers Gunter, age 15

I used to have a few porcelain dolls and I started thinking about what life might be like as a doll – fragile and pretty boring. So I wrote about a doll who strays too far out of bounds.

Dolls

I am a porcelain doll, ever breaking away. I finally found a way out of my cellophane wraps, with painted eyes shining like rock candy diamonds inlaid in a face of sheer perfection. Fat childish hands pull drawstrings to hear my faded whirring and recorded laughs.

My blond curls of synthetic hair bounce behind me as I walk to the edge of the shelf. My tiny crippled body looks out over the darkness of the unknown. My pink silk heart dares me to jump from my confines, to inquire what is beyond my vision. My union with the floor is sealed by a tinkling shatter as my body makes its way into pieces. The other dolls chance a look over the edge of the shelf, tears of warm sink water dropping from their saddened faces. They put up a ruckus of tears and wails, disturbing the old velveteen rabbit from his sleep. With a cough of dust, he says, "Those who are bold enough to step off the edge, fall prey to their own curiosity."

Write late at night and early in the morning, just before and after sleep. This is when your best ideas will come.

Dilcia Aviles, age 15

I wrote this poem as if I were a flower.

I Lie on the Ground Feeling the Earth Move

I lie on the ground feeling the earth move.
The grass pierces me,
prickling my skin as the
translucent sun washes over my
rose petal cheeks.

I smile
at the sun that yearns to beam on me –
to shine its rays along my spine
as I dig myself deeper,
bragging about my aromatic self
as I lie on the ground feeling the earth move.

The candlelit night stirs silently
rocking the moon in place.
The winter breeze embraces us
kissing our stems softly
lulling us to sleep.

The ocean of stars twinkle.
My embodied leaves
leave me alone
as I spread my arms
with glee in morning dew.
I lie on the ground feeling the earth move,
tired of its daily cycles.

Brianna Mitchell, age 13

I wrote this poem at a WriteGirl Workshop where we were supposed to describe objects on the table. I chose the Life Saver mint.

Crunch

Tear the wrapper –
crunch, suck
then repeat. The smell of
a Life Saver, my life saver
curing the epidemic of bad breath.
Crunch.
The white candy dissolves.
Crunch.
The last bit
melts away –
I exhale
a minty
fresh
breath.

Charice Barleta, age 17

Gothic Romanticism, as well as the show "House," inspired this poem. The character decides to reject lifesaving treatments because she doesn't want to suffer anymore. I wrote the piece from the perspective of the bruise.

Bruises

Purple as I am,
I surface unexpectedly.
She once lived to create;
impossibilities, she eliminated.
Then I conquered her body,
intoxicated by the ripe wine.
Organic is what I am.
Artificial cure, rejected.
She still bruises at the sight of pain.
She doesn't heal.
She doesn't heal.
She chooses to shut her system down.
Her pigment will soon be lost;
But the purple will live on.

Writing Experiment: Shoes' Views

Your shoes carry you into your world. They have been with you to public events and private moments. What would your shoes say if they could tell some of your stories? What have they seen? Select a pair of your shoes and let them write about their perspective on things. It can be helpful to pick up those shoes and really look them over - take a moment to remember the people and events that your shoes have visited. (If nothing really flows, try a different pair of shoes - some shoes have more stories than others!)

Kezia Obasi, age 13

At a WriteGirl Workshop, a guest speaker showed us a pair of red sneakers and asked us to write about them.

I Love You...From the Bottom of My Sole

Ah, yes, I remember the day that our love affair began. It was back-to-school week at Journey's shoe store. You came in with your mother. I knew from the moment I laid my rubber on you it was love at first sight.

I was a lonely pair of fiery red Chucks that had just been shipped to California from New York. And you were a young girl desperately looking for designer shoes. It was perfect. Well, at least I thought it was going to be. If only someone would have warned me about those brutal hours of P.E. ahead. Oh, and don't get me started on the day when your friends dared you to run into that huge, muddy puddle. I was filthy and soaked the whole day and you were too lazy to clean me. I can still taste the minty gum you hid on the bottom of my leather so you wouldn't get caught chewing it by Mr. Blubber-gut in English class!

Just so you're aware, I absolutely hate when you squeeze my tongues so tight it chokes me, and it cuts off your circulation, too. You know, sometimes I feel I'm just some object you can write all over when you're bored in second period.

Rachel Burdorf, age 16

Shoe's Views

REPORTSHOE: Mr. Nike, welcome to Shoe's Views, where we get the real story behind the abuse of the downtrodden.

JOE NIKE: Call me Joe. And you got that right. She takes me for granted. I walk her around all day, on asphalt and that cursed Astroturf, with those awful rubber bits.

REPORTSHOE: Joe, not to be unsupportive, but isn't that your job?

JOE NIKE: Yes! But after I walk her home, she forgets me! She almost never puts me with my family. She leaves me on the carpet. Carpets are bullies. They laugh at you, tickle you with their yarn and snicker. Once in a while, though, I get to dump Astroturf bits on them.

REPORTSHOE: Your local carpet sounds awful, but at least you can strike back against your worst antagonist.

JOE NIKE: Oh, I'd give my lace tips to have carpet be my worst problem. Ya see, sometimes she leaves me on the carpet under a pile of clothes! Clothes are emotionally insecure.They're always challenging you and trying to provoke arguments, but they will do anything for compliments - except shut up.

REPORTSHOE: Yeah, I feel you.

JOE NIKE: You know, it wouldn't be so bad if she didn't remove the socks. We have common ground since we're both squashed all day. Socks may not be the shiniest shoes on the rack, but we can be indignant together about our treatment.

REPORTSHOE: I've kept contact with one pair of plain seamless for longer than I care to say!

JOE NIKE: You know, being forgotten really pulls my laces! I give her stupid, pampered feet protection and cushioning, and she can't even put me to sleep with my family!

REPORTSHOE: Thank you, Joe. You've raised several important issues. Well, that's all we have time for today, but join us again for more Shoe's Views!

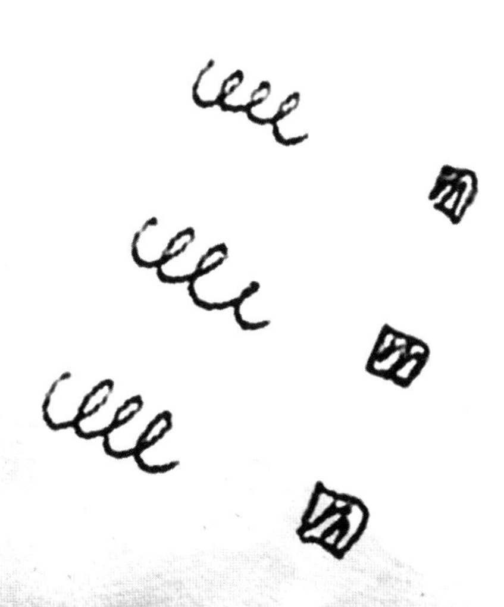

Write dialogue so that the reader knows immediately which character is speaking.

Jessica Reben, age 17

During the WriteGirl Fiction Workshop, we were asked to write about our shoes and what they might think of us. My shoes don't like me that much.

The Shoe Fit

I'm so tired, and when I'm tired, I like to give you blisters. Why must you walk so much? Get a car, or at least a bicycle. Two years has been enough. And why is there a bleach stain on me, when you were only bleaching your shoelaces? How come you never bleach me, or even wash me? I'm the one who can still smell that dog poo you stepped in a year ago. Are you trying to wear me out and get rid of me? Are you trying to get your mom to buy a new pair of shoes? Why don't you love me!? Don't you remember all of our good times, like the time we went to Six Flags twice in two weeks? All the boys you sat next to said, "Oh, nice shoes." I got you those boys. And what about Ricky? I accidentally stepped on his foot, and you ended up hitting it off and I got you Ricky. Please don't throw me away. I still have miles to go.

Zoe Camp, age 14

Black Peace Converse Point of View

Dirty. Tattered. Barely ever cleaned. I live in her closest most of my life because her mother believes I am the cause of her fractured foot. I love the smile she gets when she slips her mismatched socks into the soles of my material. We run through the rain as mud and grass particles surround my rubber lining. The mud covers my laces when she kicks the dirty soccer ball at the chain-linked fence, alone during P.E. I feel the soft, muddy grass as she runs with all her might to keep up with her class. She curls her toes when he kisses her. She stands on the tips of her toes when he hugs her. The black material and colorful peace signs touch his black leather converses, as he taps on her feet when they are across from each other. The adventures we've shared. All the memories. From the first kiss to our first plane flight across the world. When my last day comes and the soles of my material are broken and I am ripped to shreds, I will remember her smile as she pulls me on and ties the dirty, tattered strings she calls laces.

Writing Experiments

(Excerpted from the WriteGirl Publication, *Pens on Fire: Creative Writing Experiments for Teens from WriteGirl.*)

Here are a variety of writing experiments guaranteed to get your ink flowing. Try a new one every Saturday, or when you are doing laundry, or every time you are standing in line somewhere. Be your own mentor - encourage yourself to write often and be bold.

SCREENWRITING EXPERIMENTS

Talk to Yourself

Write a scene between you - and you. Choose yourself now and your 70-year-old self. Or choose yourself now and your seven-year-old self.

> *Put your 70-year-old self in a city, location or situation that you would never imagine yourself being in today. People change - ask your future self what brought him/her there.*

Action Speaks Louder

When you write a scene, what your characters DO can say as much as their words. Write a scene focusing on your characters' actions. Does a character simply turn away instead of answering a question? Start flipping channels on the TV to avoid a fight instead of just yelling? Punch a wall?

> *Close your eyes and have someone read your scene out loud. What do you see your characters doing? Now have someone else with a completely different voice and style of speaking read the scene. Do you see your characters acting differently?*

Odd Buddies

Think of two friends that have NOTHING in common. Now force them to do an activity together, like solve a crime or make a peanut butter sandwich. (The movie term for this is "buddy" or if it's funny, "buddy comedy.")

Sketch it out (stick figures are fine!). Think of a comic book or a sketch for a cartoon. Look for physical comedy.

CREATIVE NONFICTION EXPERIMENTS

The Scoop on Your Family

Write a paragraph about a family member you see often. Write about their day, their routine or simply how they are at the dinner table.

Use all your senses! As you write, think about how things smell, sound, feel, taste and look. Give us your complete experience.

Not Just Business

Pick a business that you walk or drive past every day. It may be a place you've been curious about or a place you've barely noticed. Interview the owner or manager about the company's history. See if you can find out its ties to the community or any information you think people would be surprised to know.

How much do you know about what your parents or friends' parents do? Interview one of them. Ask specific questions that elicit visual images of the tasks required by their type of work.

Share your work – join a writers group.

Read All About It

Write about your life in headlines only. First, give your newspaper a name. Then, write the headlines for every section of the newspaper.

> *Put the newspaper together! Cut out all your headlines and arrange them on several large pieces of paper. What headline do you put at the top? What order do you put them in? What headlines are missing? Add a few more to complete your paper.*

Tell Them What You REALLY Think

There's someone you need to say something to. If you were to sit down and write them a letter right now, who would you write to? What do you want to tell this person? What is your intention in writing? You don't need to mail it, but definitely start writing it now.

> *Try writing this in a different genre – as a song, a screenplay, a radio jingle, an excerpt from a historical nonfiction novel...*

JOURNALISM EXPERIMENTS

Profile Yourself

Write a paragraph about who you are; write it in the third-person (as if you were the journalist writing this story about someone else).

> *Ask your friends, families, teachers or mentors to be a "source" for your piece. Interview them – and write down direct quotes from each of them to include in your profile.*

Leaky Faucet

Make a list of things you don't like in your home (early curfew, noisy brothers and sisters, no television, too hot or cold) and write an editorial about the things that frustrate you about your living situation. Try to keep your tone and style consistent, whether it's comedic, dramatic or irritated.

Now report on what you imagine your parent's, sibling's, or pet's pet peeves are, using the same level of detail with which you wrote about your own. What kinds of observations overlap? Contrast?

Talk the Talk

The art of the interview is key for a reporter. Find an area in which a friend or family member is an expert and interview him/her about it. (Remember to let him/her ramble a bit – that leads to some good stuff.)

Do some research! Look up interviews online or in magazine and books to find different kinds of questions to ask. Sometimes you get the best material from your subjects through uncommon inquiries!

Not!

Write an editorial expressing an opinion you passionately believe in. Now write it again, taking the opposite side. Your goal is to be every bit as passionate and convincing this time.

Write the second part of this exercise in a completely different locale than you did the first. For example, if you were in your bedroom initially, go to a park and write the rebuttal on a bench, or sit on the grass under a tree.

Use dialogue to develop characters, not just to give information about the plot.

Trash or Treasure?

Find a piece of paper in your pocket or backpack. It could be a receipt, a movie ticket stub, a wrapper... Tape it onto a page in your journal. Write down what it says about you. Give all the details.

Imagine it could talk to you. What would it say?

Break Your Patterns

Write with a different pen than you usually use, a crayon or charcoal. Write in a spiral, upside-down, around the edges, over top of a picture, in HUGE letters or in tiny, tiny writing...see how your writing changes when you change things around.

Write in the dark! Don't worry about straight lines or crossing your Ts. Just let yourself go!

I Am a Goldfish

Imagine waking up in the morning as a kind of animal. What kind of animal are you? Write a story about your day as you go about your normal activities as this animal, and show how your family and friends would react.

Put a journal next to your bed and record what kind of animal you feel like every morning for a week, including why. Do your notes change from day to day? What kind of animal do you feel like before you go to sleep at night? Is it the same as in the morning?

Dear Prudence

Sometimes people start journal entries with "Dear Diary." Try starting off a journal entry with "Dear...somebody." You choose. It can be somebody fictional or real - a relative, a friend, an imaginary friend when you were three years old or somebody famous (living or dead).

Imagine you are the "somebody" that the journal entry was meant for and write a response.

What's In a Name?

Write about your name: first name, last name, middle name, nickname, names you were almost called, names you wish you were or weren't called, etc. We all have powerful feelings about our names.

Get specific. How does each syllable sound? Do you have hard consonants like Ks and Bs? Or do you have lots of soft and rolling letters like Rs and Ls? Something in the middle like Ss? What would you call yourself if you could give yourself a whole new name, and why?

Go with the Flow

Brainstorm: Open up your journal and write down everything that comes to your mind for the next five minutes. You might find yourself continually jumping to new thoughts, or you might find that there's one topic on your mind that is compelling you. Keep your pen going.

Do this everyday at the same time (when you wake up, as you are on the bus going to school, immediately after dinner, etc.) for at least 7 days. Does it feel easier to keep writing on the 7th day? Keep this habit of writing every day for as long as possible. Every writer needs practice.

Always write more than two drafts.

FICTION EXPERIMENTS

Pull Out the Gloves

Think of a major fight you have had with someone or make one up. Remember the details of it and then write it as a scene from the other person's point of view. What emotions would have prompted them to act and talk as they did?

Some of the most meaningful aspects of conversations lie in what is not said, rather than what is said. After you've finished your first draft, remove everything but the dialogue. Are there redundancies? Does each character have an authentic style of speaking? Does the dialogue truly capture their emotions?

Trade Places

Try writing a journal entry as if you are someone else - maybe the guy sitting a few tables away at the coffee shop where you write, a character from a story you're working on, the President, your best friend, your worst enemy, a teacher, your favorite author while they were writing your favorite book or an athlete before a big game.

To help yourself get into the mind of someone else, try a beverage you have never had before, put on an unfamiliar hat or piece of jewelry, or act as if you are a foot taller (or shorter) than you are.

POETRY EXPERIMENTS

My Best Friend Is Like a Hamburger

Compare someone who inspires you to an object, event or place in your everyday life. Give us details about how they are the same and how they are different.

Think of both physical and metaphorical objects. Try different objects for the same person to see which fits best.

No Peeking

Close your eyes for one minute and take in all the non-visual stimuli. Now write a poem about what you just experienced – the way your breath feels moving through your body, the conversation you just overheard, the way coffee smells waft past. Write about all the things you noticed.

Do this five times throughout the day in different locations.

Five by Five

Give yourself word limits. For example, write a poem about the last time you laughed or cried really hard, using only five lines and five words per line. Sometimes freedom can come from restriction.

Read your words slowly, thoughtfully. Are these the best words you can use to fit your emotion, experience, etc? Revise your writing, allowing yourself to add or delete only one word per line.

I Used To...

Write a poem with each line filling in the blanks of "I used to be _____ but now I am ______." ("I used to write poems, but now I just do experiments."; "I used to be afraid of spiders, but now I just look at them with curiosity.")

Make a list of these sentences being completely truthful, then make another list of these sentences but just write them as utter fiction. Be as nonsensical and fantastical as possible!

Big Ears

Write a poem consisting entirely of overheard conversation.

Add in your responses to what people have said.

Tribute Song

Take a famous song and change the lyrics to make it a "tribute song." Pick someone you know, who has a birthday or anniversary coming up and re-write the lyrics using funny and specific things about that person, or pet, or whomever.

If you're having a tough time matching the lyrics to a tune, you could also make up your own simple melody.

A Perfect Day

Imagine a perfect day in your childhood. What happened that day to make it memorable? Picture yourself back there: What is the weather like? The temperature, the breeze, the clouds – how does your skin feel? What are the smells? What are you wearing? Who else is there? How is her/his hair fixed – what is his/her scent? What are the sounds around you? How about taste? Engage all your senses in creating the image. When you look at what you have written, is there a center to your images? What overarching image sets the theme? What phrase could capture that central image? Now you have the nugget from which a song might flow

Writing songs is similar to writing fiction – you start with something you know and let the story/scene take you to new places. Get to know your songs and characters and don't hesitate to turn your piece into something fictional!

ESSAY WRITING EXPERIMENTS

My Future

Write a brief (three paragraphs) autobiography of your future! Be sure to include a title.

Let loose! Expriment with irony and innuendo in your essay writing. How could this examination be more humorous?

This Inspires Me

It's not all about classic literature and music – modern art forms are important, and influential too! Which piece, from a musical, visual or literary artist still creating today, do you admire most? What is it about their work that you connect with? Do you think it will stand the test of time? Write a 200-word essay about the piece.

Try writing this piece from the perspective of the object you chose. Evaluate why people value you today, and why they will continue to value you even as times change.

I Am Home

Where is your home? It could be a building, a state of mind, a gathering of people, a landscape or a feeling that comes over you when you know you're there. Write a 300-word essay about what home means to you.

If you're stuck, think about your friends' and relatives' homes. How is your experience there different than in your own home? Can you now define what specifically defines "home" for you?

writegirl

These are but wild and
writegirl
www.writegirl.org

This is WriteGirl

Founded in 2001, WriteGirl is a creative writing and mentoring organization that promotes creativity, critical thinking and leadership skills to empower teen girls. WriteGirl currently serves over 300 at-risk teen girls in Los Angeles County.

In its Core Mentoring Program, with participants drawn from more than 60 schools, WriteGirl pairs at-risk teen girls with professional women writers for one-on-one mentoring, workshops, public readings and publication in award-winning, nationally-distributed anthologies. WriteGirl also provides individual college and financial aid guidance to every participant. For the ninth year in a row, 100% of teens participating in the Core WriteGirl Mentoring Program have graduated high school and enrolled in college.

WriteGirl alumni Rachel Hogue, First Lady Maria Shriver and WriteGirl Executive Director Keren Taylor, receiving the award for the 2010-11 California Nonprofit of the Year.

First Lady Maria Shriver, Keren Taylor and Governor Arnold Schwarzenegger

Photo: Steven Hellon

TV writer Elizabeth Sarnoff (*Lost*) offers writing advice

WriteGirl mentors are novelists, poets, journalists, songwriters and more.

This anthology is the ninth publication from WriteGirl's Core Mentoring Program.

WriteGirl also brings weekly creative writing workshops to critically at-risk teen girls at schools in Azusa, Compton, Lawndale, Pico Rivera, South Los Angeles and Rampart in its innovative In-Schools Program. In the past two years, the In-Schools Program has expanded to serve 150 girls at six schools, including three Los Angeles County Office of Education (LACOE) Alternative Education Cal-SAFE Schools and a LACOE Community Day School site. Cal-SAFE (California School Age Family Education) schools are state-supported educational programs that serve pregnant and parenting minors. Community Day Schools specifically target student populations deemed the most at risk. Students at these schools are pregnant or parenting teens, foster youth, on probation, have social workers or are unable to return to their home schools due to any number of issues. WriteGirl also provides an In-Schools Program at New Village Charter School.

Through participation in the WriteGirl In-Schools Program, students develop vital communication skills, self-confidence, critical thinking skills, deeper academic engagement and enhanced creativity for a lifetime of increased opportunities.

Today I enjoyed the freedom to just imagine and write.

Mentoring

WriteGirl matches professional women writers with teen girls for one-on-one mentoring in creative writing. Every week, mentoring pairs write at a coffee shops or libraries. They laugh, explore, create, reflect and inspire each other. WriteGirl selects and trains women writers to become writing mentors, and Mentor Advisors provide support and help throughout the year. 150 women writers contribute 2,000 volunteer hours each month as mentors, workshop leaders and volunteers.

Pairs work together for the nine-month season, and many return year after year. The average participation in the WriteGirl Core Mentoring Program is three years.

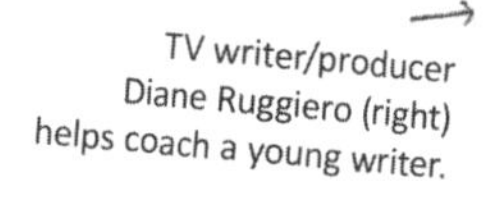

TV writer/producer Diane Ruggiero (right) helps coach a young writer.

My mentee is a creative wonder, and I am inspired by who she is, and who she is becoming: an articulate, beautiful, notable, amazing writer.

Seeing these students grow has encouraged my own writing, reminding me that we all have a story to tell.

Mentors guide girls through the college research and application process. In each of our nine seasons, 100% of our participating seniors have gone on to college.

Mentors help girls to write, edit and perform their creative work, and in the process, the mentors' own writing is re-invigorated.

Workshops

WriteGirl teens and women writers gather one Saturday each month for a full day of writing. Workshops are led by professional women poets, screenwriters, songwriters, novelists and journalists – some of the most respected writers in their fields.

We experiment!

Workshops incorporate objects, music, newspapers, posters, props, scents and other interactive components. ↙

We write it down! ↖

Many of the pieces found in this book started out as WriteGirl workshop experiments.

←

We act up!

At the Screenwriting Workshop, Oscar- and Emmy Award-winning writers, directors and actors come together to perform and discuss WriteGirl scenes & monologues written throughout the day. Here, screenwriter Nancy Meyers (*It's Complicated*) offers writing help.

WriteGirl is a place where I can express myself freely and without judgment. I can get my point across any way I want to.

We sing out!

At the Songwriting Workshop, some of the best-known songwriters in the country are on hand to demonstrate the ins and outs of lyric writing, and set the girls' lyrics to music – right on the spot! ↓

←

We speak up!

WriteGirl teens express themselves, by sharing their work, and by taking a turn on the workshop "soap box."

We congregate! →

Through group activities and over lunch donated by local restaurants, we get to know each other as writers and friends.

WriteGirl workshops leave me feeling transcendent, allowing me greater perspective on what I see within myself and of what I sense within the rest of the world.

Special Guest Presenters and Mentors

Screenwriting Workshop:

Writers:

Gina Prince-Bythewood
Sarah Fain
Naomi Foner
Nancy Meyers
Diane Ruggiero
Elizabeth Sarnoff

Actors:

Sean Michael Boozer
Sprague Grayden
Pamela Hayden
Porter Kelly
Joel McCrary
Kim McCullough
Edi Patterson
Retta Putignano
Robin Weigert
Nora Zehetner

Screenwriter Naomi Foner (*Bee Season*) guides a young writer.

Actors joined us to perform scenes and monologues written that day.

I've forgotten what it's like to sit in the environment of bright women who cheer each other on.

Songwriting Workshop:

Louise Goffin
Kate Hanley
L.P.
Michelle Lewis
Lisa Loeb
Eve Nelson
Pam Sheyne
Renee Stahl
Rosemarie Tan

Poetry Workshop:

Kim Dower
Suzanne Lummis
Pat Payne
Dorothy Randall Gray
Patricia Seyburn

Poet Patty Seyburn talks about objects as inspiration.

Fiction/Nonfiction Workshop:

Lesley Balla
Sherri L. Smith
Margaret Stohl
Lindsay William-Ross

Performance Workshop:

B.J. Dodge

Journalism Workshop:

Jennifer Quinonez
Alexandra Zavis

Songwriters Michelle Lewis, Lisa Loeb and Renee Stahl share secrets of writing lyrics.

Literary Panel:

Betsy Amster
Laurel Ann Bogen
Kim Dower
Linda Friedman
Ida Ziniti

Public Readings

WriteGirl teens read their work boldly at bookstores and book festivals all over the city. Their voices entertain and inspire audiences of friends, family and newcomers to WriteGirl.

They read straight from their journal, a single piece of paper or from a WriteGirl anthology. Their words inspire other women and girls to join WriteGirl.

For many of the girls, it's the first time they've ever read their words in public.

The WriteGirl nine-month season culminates in a special reading event at the Writers Guild of America Theater in Beverly Hills, complete with a silent auction, reception, special celebrity guests and a sneak preview of the next WriteGirl anthology.

WriteGirls encourage each other to take chances in their work.

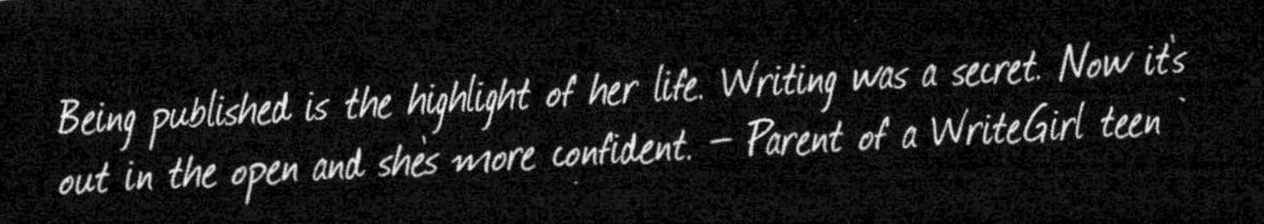

Bold Ink Awards

The WriteGirl Bold Ink Awards were created four years ago to honor the women who inspire our girls, our mentors and audiences around the world. We seek out storytellers whose voices move us. Their genres represent the breadth of our own membership and their achievements mark the degree of excellence we all strive for. They write in **Bold Ink**.

Presenters included actress Robin Weigert, *Los Angeles Times* Book Editor David Ulin, screenwriter/director Robin Swicord and California Poet Laureate Carol Muske-Dukes.

2010 Honorees:
TV writer/Executive Producer Elizabeth Sarnoff;
author/entrepreneur Lynda Resnick;
fiction writer Marisa Silver;
poet Patricia Seyburn; and
screenwriter/director Nancy Meyers.

It's always interesting to see what happens when a group of women are in one room together, armed with pen and paper.

Flowers donated by Teleflora; food contributed by Stefan's at L.A. Farm; drinks from POM, Barefoot Wine & Bubbly and Mumm Napa.

Past Bold Ink Award Honorees:

Wanda Coleman, Jennifer Crittenden, Diablo Cody, Liz Craft, Sarah Fain, Janet Fitch, Carol Flint, Naomi Foner, Gigi Levangie, Callie Khouri, Suzanne Lummis, Patt Morrison, Carol Muske-Dukes, Sonia Nazario, Gina Prince-Bythewood, Carolyn See, Mona Simpson, Jill Soloway, Robin Swicord, Sandra Tsing Loh and Diane Warren.

Publications

Since 2001, WriteGirl Publications has been producing award-winning anthologies that showcase the bold voices and imaginative insights of women and girls. Unique in both design and content, WriteGirl anthologies present a wide range of personal stories, poetry, essays, scenes and lyrics, as well as a selection of WriteGirl writing experiments to inspire readers to find their own creative voices.

Nine anthologies from WriteGirl showcase the work of over 1,000 women and girls. Selections range from serious to whimsical, personal to political, and heart-rending to uplifting.

WriteGirl anthologies have collectively won 26 national and international book awards. You should see the medals and certificates adorning our office!

Order WriteGirl books online from www.WriteGirl.org, from www.Amazon.com, or buy them in person from dozens of bookstores nationwide.

ForeWord Reveiws, School Library Journal, Kirkus, Los Angeles Times Book Reveiw, The Writer Magazine and *VOYA* have all raved about WriteGirl books.

"WriteGirl's wonderful, inspirational anthology [*Listen to Me*] belongs in every media center, public library and creative writing class."
– VOYA Magazine Review

"Until girls from around the country can access the beauty in one-on-one mentoring and a varied writing education, each anthology from WriteGirl offers a small taste of the experience."
– ForeWord Magazine Review

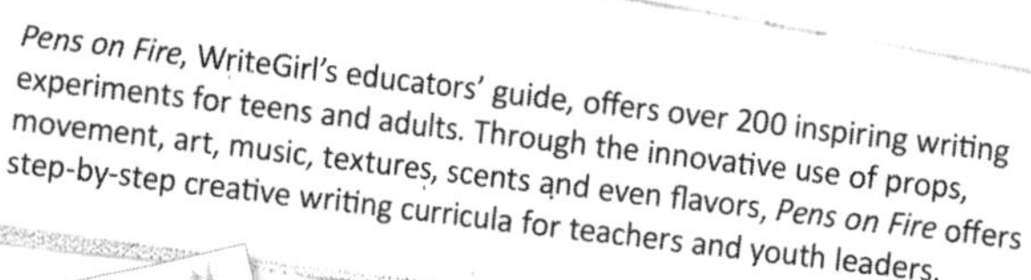

Pens on Fire, WriteGirl's educators' guide, offers over 200 inspiring writing experiments for teens and adults. Through the innovative use of props, movement, art, music, textures, scents and even flavors, *Pens on Fire* offers step-by-step creative writing curricula for teachers and youth leaders.

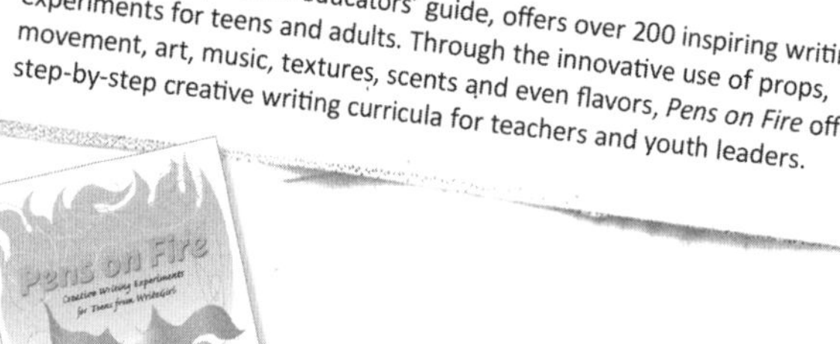

"I've searched everywhere on the Internet and at teachers' fairs for something like this to help me make creative writing fun and interesting for my class. *Pens on Fire* is amazing!"
– Mark Taylor, LAUSD Teacher of the Year 2008

WriteGirl books have collectively won 26 national and international book awards.

Find our books online at www.WriteGirl.org and www.Amazon.com

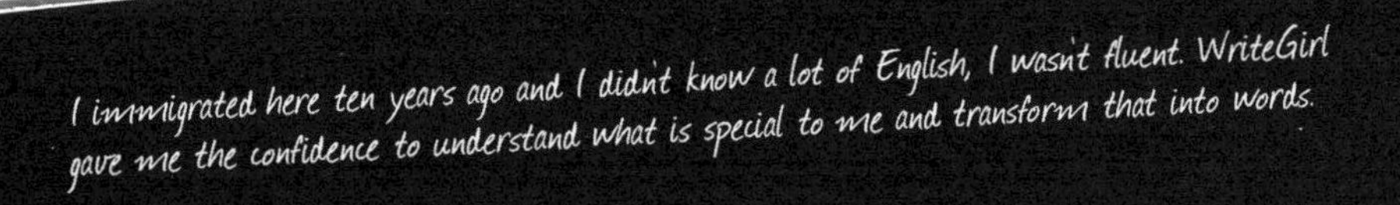

WriteGirl made me want something different: to grow as an individual, to start fresh, to see how much more I can change and grow.

Youth Leadership

WriteGirl develops leaders. We never underestimate the power of a girl and her pen.

WriteGirl teens help in leadership roles – they lead writing workshops, plan events, produce content for the WriteGirl blog, assess programming, serve as organizational spokespeople and more.

www.writegirlblog.wordpress.com

WriteGirl teens have won creative writing awards from Mayor Antonio Villaraigosa, the City of Los Angeles Department of Cultural Affairs and The Sally Picow Foundation.

WriteGirl teens have been awarded guest writing spots at the *Huffington Post Blog* and *Wall Street Journal* and internships at the *Los Angeles Times*, The Getty Museum and the LA Opera.

WriteGirl instilled in me the idea that I can succeed if I put my mind to it and kept me from straying from my plan of going to college.

I have an unquenchable desire to succeed – that is why I want my sister to join WriteGirl.

WriteGirl teens have been awarded scholarships from numerous colleges as well as The Posse Foundation and The Minerva Leadership Program as part of The Women's Conference, presented by First Lady of California Maria Shriver. WriteGirl teens were also featured panelists at the Geena Davis Institute for Gender in Media Conference and The Momentum Awards presented by the Women's Foundation of California.

Leadership: The WriteGirl "Engine"

Executive Director
Keren Taylor

Associate Director
Allison Deegan

Events and Operations
Reparata Mazzola

Membership Coordinator
Ali Prosch

In-Schools Coordinators
Diana Rivera
Katherine Thompson

Workshop Coordinator
Kirsten Giles

Administrative Assistant
Kiran Puri

Public Relations
Rachel Wimberly

Event Assistants
Claire Baker
Naomi Buckley
Carey Campbell
Cindy Collins
Ellen Giurelo
Allison Longton
Stephanie Simpson

Interns
Nataly Chavez
Rachel Jamieson
Zoe Young

High School Interns
Special thanks to the Constitutional Rights Foundation for the placement and supervision of committed teens interning with WriteGirl.
Alma Castrejon
Yvonne Ha
Stephanie Hernandez
May Quach

Website, Branding, Book Design, Graphics
Sara Apelkvist
Amanda Charles
Juliana Sankaran-Felix
Vince Serecin
design{makes me}happy.

Special Events
Retta Putignano *(Silent Auction Chair)*
Linda Folsom *(Team Leader)*
Alyson Beecher
Jeanine Cornillot
Jane Gov
Julie Haire
Kendra Kozen
Carly Milne
Sarah Wise

Book Publicity
Christine Bevins *(Team Leader)*
Julia Drake
Emma Fletcher
Brittany Michelson
Marni Rader
Krysta Whittemore

Public Relations
Rachel Wimberly *(Team Leader)*
Cindy Collins
Kim Genkinger
Margot Gerber
Pamela Hayden
Porter Kelly
Raechel Leone
Meghan Lewit
Margo McCall
Sandra O'Briant
Katy Parks Wilson
Katie Petersen
Jennifer Rustigian
Bonita Thompson
Rachel Torres

Fundraising Support
Keren Taylor *(Team Leader)*
Porschia Baker
Erica Blodgett
Sarah Burghauser
Francey Carley
Judy Fox
Mimi Freedman
Margaret Hyde
Elline Lipkin
Claudia Melatini
Maureen Moore
Elda Pineda
Laura Spain
Betsy Sullivan
Zahirah Washington
Tanisha White
Natalie Zimmerman

WriteGirl Blog
Kiran Puri *(Team Leader)*
Bonnie Gillepsie
Anthea Raymond
Kristen Waltman

Education Support
Allison Deegan *(Team Leader)*
Ami Anobi
Carol Bathke
Katie Bishop
Rebecca Cathcart
Sharon Chinn
Jia-Rui Chong Cook
Irene Daniel
Ruby Ferm
Susanne Ferrull
Carol Forbes
Claudia Forestieri
Kate Garsson
Erika Hayasaki
Alison Hills
Brande Jackson
Rhonda Johnson
Cowy Kim
Shanté Lanay
Huong Nguyen
Jazmin Ortega
Stephanie Parent
Marytza Rubio
Chelsea Steiner
Johanna Tran

Central Support
Kiran Puri *(Team Leader)*
Angie Bradshaw
Anita Brenner
Hunter Phillips
Skylar Sutton

In-Schools Program Volunteers
who work with at-risk girls at six alternative education sites: Azusa Cal-SAFE, Bermudez Cal-SAFE, Destiny Girls Academy, Hope Cal-SAFE, La Vida West Cal-SAFE and New Village Charter High School

Diana Rivera *(In-Schools Coordinator)*
Katherine Thompson *(In-Schools Coordinator)*
Sasha Ali
Claire Baker
Porschia Baker
Angie Bradshaw
Yangok Chu
Beverly Dennis
Kathleen DiPerna
Rachel Fain
Erika Hayasaki
Laura Hightower
Alison Hills
Brande Jackson
Jacqueline Jaffe
Shanté Lanay
Marlene Leach
Meghan Lewit
Celine Malanum
Lynn Maleh
Brittany Michelson
Erin Miller
Orly Minazad
Stephanie Parent
Katy Parks Wilson
Janae Patino
Amanda Pendolino
Nichole Perkins
Sharie Radin Palatt
Marytza Rubio
Katherine Satorious
Clare Sera
Laura Spain
Kit Steinkellner
Lisa Stern

Workshop Content
Kirsten Giles *(Team Leader)*
Maia Akiva
Natasha Billawala
Kathleen Cecchin
Rachel Fain
Linda Folsom
Trina Gaynon
Molly Hennessy-Fiske
Laura Hoopes
Ashaki Jackson
Jacqueline Jaffe
Michelle Lewis
Lindsay Nelson
Jennifer Oldham
Jazmin Ortega
Jackie Parker
Amanda Pendolino
Natalie Poston
Darby Price
Laura Rhinehart
Clare Sera
Kit Steinkellner
Barbara Stimson
Dana Stringer
Melissa Wong

Membership
Ali Prosch *(Team Leader)*
Abby Anderson *(Mentor Advisor)*
Kate Garsson
Jane Gov *(Mentor Advisor)*
Pamela Hayden
Mona Holmes-Nisker *(Mentor Advisor)*
Lauren Johnson
Pamela Levy
Maureen Moore
Lindsay Nelson
Jackie Parker
Teresa Rochester *(Mentor Advisor)*
Jody Rosen-Knower
Rachel Torres *(Mentor Advisor)*
Melissa Wong *(Mentor Advisor)*

Additional Support Volunteers
Bonnie Berry LaMon
Irene Daniel
Jeanine Daniels
Kristen Daniels
Tina Dupuy
Elaine Dutka
Ariel Edwards-Levy
Faith England
Claudia Forestieri
Deborah George
Jazmine Green
Rebecca Jupiter
Tanja Laden
Lindey Lambert
Marlene Leach
Jacqueline Lesko
Darby Lewis
Michelle Maher
Sandy Matke
Mary O'Malley
Patricia Oropeza
Kathy Palagonia
Nandita Patel
Natalie Poston
Audra Quinn
Emily Richmond
Pamela Russell
Beth Schacter
Alicia Sedwick
Carla Simone
Stephanie Sorensen
Chelsea Steiner
Dana Valenzuela
Tracy Wise

WriteGirl Advisory Board

Barbara Abercrombie, Novelist, UCLA Writing Instructor, Lecturer

Shelley Berger, Poet and Teacher

Mark Bisgeier, Entertainment Attorney

Susie Coelho, Lifestyle Expert, Author and Television Host

Mark E. Cull, Author and Publisher, Red Hen Press

Paul Cummins, Executive Director, New Visions Foundation

Allison Deegan, Public Education Administrator, After School Consultant

Kai EL´ Zabar, Writer, Editor, Multimedia Consultant

Elizabeth Forsythe Hailey, Novelist

Mollie Gregory, Author, Teacher, Consultant for Writers

John Marshall, Vice President of Manufacturing, RR Donnelley, Gl Provider of Integrated Communications (Advisory Board Chair)

Vickie Nam, Writer, Editor of *Yell-Oh Girls* (Asian-American teen anthology), Interactive Producer

Maria del Pilar O'Cadiz, Ph.D., Senior Research Specialist, UC Irvine

Joy Picus, Former L.A. City Councilwoman, Community Organizer

Cecilia Rasmussen, Former Writer and Columnist, *Los Angeles Times*

Debbie Reber, Author and Consultant

Aleida Rodríguez, Poet, Editor, Educator, Translator, Publisher

Diane Siegel, Museum Educator, Community Organizer, Teacher, Los Angeles Public Library Consultant

Julia Sylva, Attorney, Former L.A. City Councilmember, President and Founding Member, National Women's Political Caucus, L.A. Metro

Keren Taylor, Songwriter, Poet, Visual Artist (WriteGirl Founder and Executive Director)

Community Connections

Participating Schools:

Abraham Lincoln High School
Anahuacalmecac High School
Animo Film and Theater Arts Charter High School
Arleta High School
Assumption of the Blessed Virgin Mary
Azusa High School
Belmont High School
Benjamin Franklin High School
Bishop Conaty-Our Lady of Lore School
Bridges Academy
Calabasas High School
CALS Early College High School
Central High School #9
Claremont High School
Covina High School
Crenshaw Arts Tech High School
Crossroads School
Culver City High School
Eagle Rock High School
Frederick Douglass High School
Foothill High School
Garfield Senior High School
George K. Porter Middle School
George Washington Preparatory High School
Glendale High School
Grant High School
Hamilton High School
Harvard Westlake School
Hawthorne Middle School
Hollywood High School
Immaculate Heart Middle School
Incarnation School
International Studies Learning Center
John Burroughs High School
John Marshall High School
John Muir Middle School
Kennedy High School
KIPP Academy of Opportunity
King Drew High School
L.A. County High School for the Arts
La Reina High School
Le Lycée Français de Los Angeles
Los Angeles Academy Middle School
Los Angeles Center for Enriched Studies
Los Angeles Leadership Academy
Manual Arts High School
Marantha High School
Mark Keppel High School
Marlborough School
Marshall High School
Miguel Contreras Learning Complex School
Northridge Academy High School
Options For Youth
Orange County High School of the Arts
Oscar de la Hoya Animo Charter High School
Palos Verdes Peninsula High School
Pasadena High School
Polytechnic High School
Port of Los Angeles High School
Ralston Intermediate School
Ramona Convent School
Renaissance High School for the Arts
Richard Merkin Middle School
Santa Monica High School

Sherman Oaks Center for Enriched Studies
Sonora High School
South Hills High School
St. Mary's High School
University High School
Verdugo Hills High School
View Park Preparatory High School
Village Glen School Westside
Walter F. Dexter Middle School
West Adams Preparatory High School
Westridge School
Ynez Middle School

Referring Organizations:
Antioch University Los Angeles
Constitutional Rights Foundation
Fox Gives
Idealist.org
Los Angeles Times Festival of Books
MLA Partner Schools
NBC Universal
PEN Center USA West
UCLA Extension Writers' Program
United Way of Ventura
USC Master of Professional Writing Program
VolunteerMatch
West Hollywood Book Fair
The Women's Conference
Writers Guild of America, West
Writers Guild of America Foundation

WriteGirl teens meet and discuss the writing process with Suzan-Lori Parks.

WriteGirl Supporters

WriteGirl would like to thank the following for their generous support.

amazon.com

WriteGirl is grateful to Amazon.com for its grant in support of the publication of this anthology.

Foundations and Corporations:

Adams Family Foundation
Ahmanson Foundation
America Association of University Women
American University School of Communication
Annenberg Foundation
Band From TV
BLT & Associates
Boone Family Foundation
City of Los Angeles Cultural Affairs Department, Youth Arts and Education Program
Diane Warren Foundation
DIRECTV
Disney Worldwide Outreach
Dwight Stuart Youth Foundation
Edlow Family Fund
FACE Stockholm
Fancifull Gift Baskets
Fox
The Green Foundation
iGive.com
J.R. Hyde III Family Foundation
Kaenon Polarized
Kikkerland
The Literary Lab
Lionsgate
Los Angeles County Office of Education
Los Angeles Unified School District - Beyond the Bell Branch
NBC Universal Foundation
Oder Family Foundation
Ralph M. Parsons Foundation
Ralphs
Realsongs
Roll International
RR Donnelley
San Gennaro Foundation
Soroptimist International
Sprinkles Cupcakes
Steve Martin Foundation
Time Warner
Weingart Foundation
Woman's Club of Hollywood
Women and Words
Women's Foundation of California
Writers Guild of America, West

Our Special Thanks to

All of our individual donors who have so generously contributed to help WriteGirl grow and help WriteGirl serve more teen girls each year

All of WriteGirl's mentors and volunteers for professional services, including strategic planning, public relations, event coordination, mentoring management, training and curriculum development, catering, financial management and administrative assistance

Advisory Board Members for their support and guidance on strategy, fundraising, communications and development of community partnerships

Governor Arnold Schwarzenegger and First Lady Maria Shriver; The Honorable Mayor Antonio Villaraigosa; Los Angeles Council members Eric Garcetti, Tom LaBonge and **Jan Perry** for their support and acknowledgement of WriteGirl's contributions to the community

Los Angeles Unified School District, Beyond the Bell and the Miguel Contreras Learning Center for providing a workshop space where over 150 women and girls gather to write each month; **Yucca Community Center, the GRAMMY Foundation Recording Academy** and **Writers Guild of America** for event space

RR Donnelley for ongoing support

Silent Auction donors, for support at our fundraising events

Book Expo America, *Los Angeles Times* Festival of Books, West Hollywood Book Fair and UCLA Writers Faire for donating WriteGirl booth space and promotional support at these events

Writing Journal Donors: Harry Abrams, Blick Art Materials, BrushDance Inc., Cavallini Papers & Co., Chronicle Books, Falling Water, Fiorentina, Flavia, Galison/MudPuppy Press, Hartley and Marks, JournalBooks, Kikkerland Design, Anne McGilvray & Company, Michael Roger Press, Mirage Paper Company, Running Rhino & Co., K. Schweitzer, Trends International, Whimsy Press

Food, Dessert and Beverages at WriteGirl Workshops and Special Events: Bagel Broker, Barefoot Wine and Bubbly, Barragan's Mexican Restaurant, Big Sugar Bakeshop, BLD, Border Grill/Ciudad, Bristol Farms, Cake Monkey, Canelé, Cannoli Kings, Chaya Restaurant Group, Cookie Casa, Corner Bakery, Frankie's on Melrose, FIJI Water, Fresh and Easy, Margaret Hyde, Granatas Italian Villa, IZZE Beverages, Johnny Carino's, Kate Mantilini's, Kychon Chicken, La Brea Bakery, Le Pain Quotidien, Little

Dom's, Los Sombreros, Lost Soul's Café, Louise's Trattoria , Mani's Bakery, Marengue Bakery, Masa of Echo Park, Michael's Restaurant, Modern Spirits, Mozza, Mumm Napa, Newman's Own, Nancy Silverton, Stefan's at L.A. Farm, Panda Restaurant Group, Panera Bread, Pescado Mojado, PitFire Pizza, Platine Cookies, POM Wonderful, Porto's Bakery, Ralph's, RAW Revolution, Señor Fish, Sharkey's Woodfire Grill, St. Urbain Street Bagels, Sweets for the Soul, SusieCakes, Tacos and Company, Trader Joe's, Tudor House, Union Bagel, Yuca's

Gifts for Members and Event Donors: ABC, Abra Therapeutics, Apothecary Fairy, Claire Baker, Blackwell Fitness, Boo Boo Bling Shop, Border Grill Santa Monica, Carolina Pads, Creative Age Publications, DIRECTV, Disney, Dr. Bronner's Magic Soaps, Earthly Body, Earthpack, EK Success, EOS, Everybody's Nuts, FACE Stockholm, Fox Searchlight, Fyred Up, Glee Gum/Verve, Glendale Laser Group, Good Cheer Company, Graphique De France, Kitsch*n Glam, Little MissMatched, Los Angeles Sparks, LuLu Belle Productions, Inc., Kikkerland, Kirana Skin Care Clinic, Klean Bath & Body, Konnect PR, Machado Art, Magnetic Poetry, Melting Pot Food Tours, Mindful Nest, Murad Skin Care Products, Nancy's Creation, Nathalie Searver Boutique, NBC/Universal, Nektar De Stagni, Neutrogena, Noodle Talk, One Coast, Oriental Trading Co., Pacific Theatres, Paula's Choice, Pickwick Bowl, Pomegranate Communications, Quotable Cards, Re-Mi Vintage, Roll, The San Brand Group, Southern California Beauty Supplies, The Story Society, Tarte, Teleflora, Tema, Two's Company, Vietrie, The Writers Junction, Zina Beverly Hills Sterling Silver

Printing and Copy Services: Chromatic Lithographers Inc., The Dot Printer, FedEx Office, RR Donnelly, Staples Copy & Print Center, Sterling Pierce Printing, Stuart F. Cooper, U-Printing

Design: Sara Apelkvist, Amanda Charles, design{makes me}happy, Julianna Parr, Ali Prosch, Juliana Sankaran-Felix, Vince Serecin (Flying Pie Design)

Photography/Videography: Tiffany Gilmore, Malcolm Gladwell, Clayton Goodfellow, Thomas Hargis, Laura Hoopes, Margaret Hyde, Mario de Lopez, Justin Rubin, Alicia Soto, Katy Parks Wilson, Rachel Wimberly, Jennifer Rustigian, Marvin Yan

Website/Branding: Fabric Interactive and **Sara Apelkvis**t for design and branding strategy, including development of WriteGirl's logo, website, press kit, stationery, publications and ongoing support

Meet the WriteGirl Mentors

Maia Akiva is a self-help fiction writer. She's originally from Israel. Her plays *Life* and *I Hate Love* are published by Brooklyn Publishers. Her short stories are published in *Bewildering Stories, Diverse Voices Quarterly* and *Spirits* literary magazine. You can find her and her writing at: www.selfhelpfiction.net.

Abby Anderson is a feature film and TV writer specializing in smart comedy. Her scripts have placed in major screenwriting contests, including as a Quarterfinalist in the Nicholl Fellowship. In 2009, Abby was one of only 40 writers selected to be a Writer-in-Residence at Hedgebrook Writers' Retreat.

As an artist, **Porschia Baker** uses words as an agency to break through herself and incite crevices in whoever is witnessing. Her work chronicles her journey and expresses her hopes. Currently, she is a student in Goddard College's M.F.A.-I.A.

Natasha Billawala always planned to work in television. She regards TiVo as one her best friends and enjoys character-driven TV shows. Working on *Buffy The Vampire Slayer* and *Everwood* are among her favorite experiences.

Anita Susan Brenner is a trial attorney in Pasadena, California. Her poems have appeared in *Puerto del Sol, PresenTense, Slipstream, Owen Wister Review, tnr, Potato Eyes* and other journals.

Teri Brown-Jackson is a native of Detroit. She started out working in news for KFWB then switched to fiction, landing her first sitcom writing job with *In the House*. Since then, it's been nothing but laughs.

Ann Carnes is an education consultant and former administrator for the Los Angeles Unified School District. Hundreds of students and teachers have benefited from her writing workshops and skillful instruction. Ann is an artist, dancer and lover of theater, and is writing her first memoir.

In Chicago, **Kathleen Cecchin** appeared onstage with several companies. In L.A., she's performed with and directed for The Attic Theatre, The Spotlight Theatre, WPOP, ALAP, LATWP and USC. You may have also seen her on NBC or CBS and can read her play *Bitch* in the collection *Can I Sit With You?*

Jia-Rui Chong Cook, a former reporter for the *Los Angeles Times*, now works in the media relations department of NASA's Jet Propulsion Laboratory, spending most of her time thinking of interesting analogies to explain Saturn. WriteGirl reminds her that there is pleasure in writing. Her travel blog is www.postmarkhere.wordpress.com.

Cindy Collins has a degree in journalism from the University of Arizona and currently writes scripts, articles, nonfiction books and short stories. This is her fourth year as a WriteGirl volunteer, and she continues to be inspired by the phenomenal young writers in this program.

An Emmy Award-winning producer, **Jeanine Cornillot** began her career as a documentary editor, and has written and produced shows for CBS, NBC, ABC and the Oprah Winfrey Network. Jeanine is also the author of *Family Sentence: The Search for My Cuban-Revolutionary, Prison-Yard, Mythic-Hero, Deadbeat Dad.*

Beverly Dennis is an academic writer, university professor and educational activist currently living in Anaheim Hills, California, with her musician husband. This is her first year as a WriteGirl volunteer.

Boston native **Kathleen DiPerna** is a television writer/producer, a freelance writer and member of the WGA. Most recently, she wrote for the Peabody and Emmy Award-winning PBS program *A Place of Our Own*. She has also worked as a jingle lyricist and a ghostwriter, and is a regular contributor to online publications and spoken word events.

Tina Dupuy is an award-winning writer, journalist and syndicated political humor columnist. She is a regular contributor to *Fast Company*. She's also covered everything from the Presidential Inauguration to Comic-Con for the *Los Angeles Times*, *Newsday*, *LA Weekly*, and *True/Slant*. Tina is the senior editor at Mediabistro's *FishbowlLA*.

Rachel Fain's second grade teacher predicted she'd be a high school dropout, because she wrote too much and, as a result, didn't finish her alphabet stories. Her teacher was wrong, and today Rachel is a writer and much better at meeting deadlines.

Susanne Ferrull has worked as a journalist, editor, publicist and freelance writer for more than 15 years. She holds a Master's degree in Magazine Journalism from Syracuse University.

In addition to being the Senior Production Executive in Walt Disney Imagineering's Media Group, **Linda Folsom** heads the WDI writers workshop, now in its sixth year, where she shares much of what she learns at WriteGirl. She's currently working on a young adult novel.

Mimi Freedman is a filmmaker who has written, produced and directed more than 50 documentary films and television programs. Her most recent project, the Turner Classic Movies documentary *Brando*, received an Emmy nomination for Outstanding Nonfiction Special.

Kate Garsson serves as an account supervisor at Ruder Finn, a global public relations agency, where she manages healthcare and technology accounts. When she's not volunteering with WriteGirl, Kate enjoys running and trying new restaurants.

After three moves in five years of marriage, **Trina Gaynon** ended up in Orange County. She persists in entering poetry contests, though the odds of winning are better playing lotto in Reno (where, by the way, she won $100).

The max word count for **Kim Genkinger**'s bio was 40. She is an Associate Creative Director/Copywriter for Fire Station, an LA-based advertising agency. So the last 20 years of her life have hinged on being able to communicate succinctly. Done.

Before coming to Los Angeles, **Kirsten Giles** lived in Kentucky, Mexico City, Honolulu, and on a small farm in northern California. When she's not creating poetry, she develops training programs and learning games for a variety of corporate clients.

Jane Gov is a writer, librarian and graduate student. Her degrees were earned primarily by making up stories. She is an avid reader and is working on a young adult novel.

Pamela Hayden is an actress and writer, best known as the voice of Milhouse on *The Simpsons*. She wrote and performed her solo show in L.A. and NYC to critical acclaim. She also received an *LA Weekly* Drama Award, and has appeared at the HBO Comedy Festival. Pamela is co-writing a musical and is honored to be a WriteGirl Gal!

Molly Hennessy-Fiske is a *Los Angeles Times* staff writer, a 1999 Harvard graduate, and a former reporter and editor at *The Harvard Crimson* and *Diversity & Distinction* magazine. She loves poetry, from Emily Dickinson to Nikki Giovanni, and crime mysteries (e.g. Agatha Christie, Patricia Cornwell and Michael Connelly).

Mona Holmes Nisker is a writer specializing in music journalism and food writing. When she's not pursuing an interview with the latest female rapper, Mona can be found at a Los Angeles restaurant or in the kitchen trying a new healthy recipe.

WriteGirl veteran **Ashaki M. Jackson** is loyal mentor to Crushtastic *Glee*-Loving Writer Ciara Blackwell. Ashaki enjoys caffè breves and Fred 62's Dime Bag special. She has studied under the tutelage of Suheir Hammad and Carl Phillips and is completing her first poetry manuscript.

Jacqueline Jaffe's short stories have appeared in numerous anthologies and literary magazines, and have been nominated for the Pushcart Prize. She teaches creative writing at several L.A. area schools and is hard at work on her M.F.A. at Antioch University.

Multi-hyphenate actress-writer-producer **Rebecca Jupiter** holds a chemistry and French degree from UC Berkeley and writes for the blog "What now? Success in L.A. after year one." She has danced onstage at Carnegie Hall and will be seen in *All Dressed Up* at the Cannes Film Festival. She is currently writing two feature films.

Porter Kelly writes and performs sketch comedy at ACME Comedy Theatre in Los Angeles. She has appeared in dozens of television commercials and teaches a class in commercial auditioning. www.porterkelly.com

Freelance teacher, author of *The Flammable Bird* and *Masque*, former 12-year Regional Director of the Poetry Society of America, Pushcart Prize Winner, Best American Poetry recipient and Literary Programs Director for The Ruskin Art Club, **Elena Karina Byrne** has work in or forthcoming in *The Paris Review, The Kenyon Review, The Yale Review, Tri Quarterly, Volt* and *Drunken Boat*.

New York native **Kendra Kozen** is an award-winning journalist whose work appears in print and online. She received a Master's degree from the University of Southern California in 2006 and has called Los Angeles home for almost a decade.

Tanja M. Laden works as a professional writer and Deputy Editor at Flavorpill L.A., and has published work in the *Los Angeles Times, Huffington Post, LA Weekly, Artillery* and other local and national outlets. She has been mentoring 17-year-old high school junior Karen Toledo for four years.

Shanté Lanay is a freelance writer and correspondent. She has written for *Honey* magazine, *Teen People* and GlobalGrind.com, and is co-author of *Organically Raised*. Shanté is also a pre-service teacher, pursuing her credential from Mount St. Mary's College. She lives in Pasadena, California with her daughter.

Michelle Lewis is one of the few resident songwriters among the WriteGirl mentors, which is why they've kept her around for the past six years. She has written songs for artists such as Lindsay Lohan, Kelly Osbourne and Josh Groban.

Pamela Levy was born in Minneapolis and spent most of her life in Los Angeles. But, being a bit of a gypsy, she has also lived in Austin and Portland. She is a legal assistant, aspiring novelist and volunteer for the City of L.A. Animal Services.

Elline Lipkin's book of poems, *The Errant Thread*, was chosen by Eavan Boland for the Kore Press First Book Award. Her second book, *Girls' Studies*, was published by Seal Press in 2009.

Celine Malanum is an L.A. native, writer and nonprofit habitué. Recently, her daughter, Pearl Luna, uttered the word "mama" and, for a moment, time stopped, the stars and heavens aligned, a ripple went through the universe and Celine's heart became new.

Laura L. Mays Hoopes is a professor of biology at Pomona College. She is working on a biography and two novels. She has published her work in the *Christian Science Monitor, North Carolina Literary Review, The Chaffin Journal, AWIS Magazine* and others.

Brooklyn-born **Reparata Mazzola** is a published author, a produced screenwriter and an Emmy-nominated television writer/producer. As a member of Barry Manilow's back-up trio, Lady Flash, she recorded on seven of his albums and toured the world. Currently, she has two screenplays in development.

Margo McCall is a graduate of the M.A. creative writing program at CSUN. Her writing has appeared in *Pacific Review, Heliotrope, Sunspinner, Toasted Cheese, Lifeboat* and other journals. She just finished *Even Now*, her first novel, and enjoys being in the creative company of WriteGirl women and girls.

Claudia Melatini is a novelist and playwright. Her play, *English Lessons*, was read at the award-winning Production Company Theatre. Her one-act, *Scrub My Tub*, was a finalist in the Summer Sizzle One-Act Play Festival. She writes for *Wine & Music*, and is a founding member of the writing group Moose Purse.

Brittany Michelson taught high school English in Arizona and English as a Second Language in Ecuador. She is working on her M.F.A. in creative writing at Antioch University. She enjoys writing nonfiction and fiction for children and young adults.

Carly Milne is a Canadian ex-pat with numerous credits in magazines, newspapers and on websites around the globe, in addition to contributing to several anthologies. Her memoir, *Sexography*, was released in 2007.

Maureen Moore is a cultural enthusiast and lover of language. She has worked extensively in Latin America and Europe, and she currently works for the Library Foundation of Los Angeles. An avid traveler, she shares her perspective on people and places through personal essays, non-fiction reflections, blog posts and op-ed pieces.

Christine Murphy Bevins has an M.F.A. in Creative Writing from Antioch University. Her essay *Mommy Maybe* was published last year. She recently completed a memoir involving love, loss and living again. She hopes to find a home for it soon.

Lindsay Nelson spent six years in Japan working as a teacher, voice actor and children's entertainer. She is currently pursuing a Ph.D. in comparative literature at USC. She has been writing since she was eight and loves helping young girls discover their own voices through WriteGirl.

With 25 years of journalism experience, including 15 years as a staff writer at the *Los Angeles Times*, **Jennifer Oldham** is known nationally as an authority on aviation travel. Oldham currently blogs at AOL's WalletPop.com and freelances for a variety of publications.

Stephanie Parent is a professional copy editor for companies including Dorchester Publishing. Her short fiction has been published in *Lady Churchill's Rosebud Wristlet* and *MARGIN: The Online Journal of Magical Realism*, and her poetry has been published in *Goblin Fruit Magazine*.

Jackie Parker, a novelist and teacher, is at work on a book about writing and community entitled *Listening to Ourselves*.

Katy Parks Wilson is a mixed media artist and photographer, and is a co-founder of Art Garage, an after-school program for preteens. She has taught creative expression to children throughout L.A. and has led teen-focused workshops with the art cooperative Art Group.

Janae Patino is a Los Angeles native who writes plays, scripts, short stories and songs. She is pursuing an M.F.A. in dramatic writing at California State University, Los Angeles.

Originally from Minnesota, **Katie Peterson** received a communications degree from Ithaca College. She works in agency PR, where she writes, conducts media relations and coordinates events for a variety of national clients. She also handles PR for her family's locavore food store.

Hunter Phillips is an award-winning UCLA M.F.A. screenwriting alum, currently working as a comedy writer at Stargreetz Inc., an entertainment and marketing company in L.A. Hunter is happy to be involved with such a worthwhile and powerful group of talented young writers.

Elda Pineda is a Los Angeles native and a writer of short stories, poetry and blogs! She is currently the Program Manager for P.S. ARTS! Her favorite writing tip is: "Keep your exclamation points under control." It's a skill she still needs to work on!

Darby Price is a New Orleans native and a poet/fiction writer. She studied creative writing at Florida State University, and has soaked up plenty of inspiration (and sunshine) in SoCal. She thinks WriteGirl is one of the best things since sliced pineapple!

In addition to her role as WriteGirl's Membership Coordinator, **Ali Prosch** works with film, video installation, sculpture and performance. She has presented a solo show at The Company (L.A.), and in group exhibits at REDCAT, Museum of Contemporary Art (Miami), Tomio Koyama Gallery (Tokyo) and White Box (NYC).

Since graduating from UCLA, **Kiran Puri** has worked with various education and arts-focused nonprofits. In addition to working as WriteGirl's Administrative Assistant, Kiran writes freelance, cooks (but never bakes), plays Spite & Malice and blogs a little, too.

Originally from Chicago, **Marietta (Retta) Putignano King** has been a WriteGirl Mentor and Silent Auction Chair for five years. She writes and performs sketch comedy and, as co-owner of Create Your Reel, writes scenes for actors' reels.

Jennifer Quinonez is an Emmy Award-winning journalist and producer for news and newsmagazine shows such as PBS's *A Place of Our Own*. Jennifer is a member of the Writers Guild of America and in 2009, won a fellowship for the RIAS Berlin German-American Exchange program for Broadcast Journalists.

A freelance writer and former brand expert for Disney and Bosch, **Marni Rader** has won national writing contests and published blogs and feature articles. She now gets her deepest literary inspirations from WriteGirls, who remind her to keep it real.

Sandra Ramos O'Briant's work has appeared in numerous journals. In addition, her short stories and essays have been anthologized in *What Wildness Is This: Women Write About the Southwest*, *Latinos in Lotus Land: An Anthology of Contemporary Southern California Literature* and *Hit List: The Best of Latino Mystery*.

Diana Rivera is a performer and writer for the theatre, an aspiring children's writer, a committed blogger, a creative coach/consultant, a featured author for Creativity Portal and an In-Schools Coordinator for WriteGirl. Her background combines teaching and curriculum development of drama, arts integration and creative writing for children and teachers.

Teresa Rochester never outgrew the "why, why, why," phase and has parlayed that into an award-winning career as a newspaper reporter. Coffee and pens are her favorite accessories. This is her fifth season as a WriteGirl mentor.

Jody Rosen Knower's work includes personal essays, profiles, book reviews, the occasional haiku and a long-running blog. She holds degrees from Columbia University Graduate School of Journalism, New York University School of Law and the University of Pennsylvania.

Marytza Rubio is a writer from Santa Ana, CA. She was a 2008 PEN USA Emerging Voices Fellow and writes about Latinas, voodoo and animals. She is also an active In-Schools volunteer at Hope Cal-SAFE.

Alicia Sedwick is an actor, writer, professor and sometime private investigator. She received her M.F.A. from American Conservatory Theatre, was an NYC-based theatre actor for many years and is also a co-producer of Spark Off Rose, a live monthly storytelling event.

A WriteGirl volunteer from day one, **Clare Sera** is a screenwriter currently working on feature film scripts for Warner Brothers, Walden Media and Disney with her writing partner, Ivan Menchell. Her award-winning short film, *Pie'n Burger,* was picked up for distribution by the Spiritual Cinema Circle and is available at Amazon.com!

This is **Barbara Stimson**'s fourth year as a mentor. In her day job, she writes computer system documentation and specifications. Outside work, her writing takes a much more creative direction, inspired by the WriteGirl workshops and weekly mentoring.

Dana L. Stringer is currently a graduate student in the M.F.A. creative writing program at Antioch University Los Angeles. She is an activist poet, playwright and spoken word artist. Her first stage play, *Kinsman Redeemer,* was produced in 2006.

Formerly a studio and production company reader and story analyst, **Bonita Thompson** is now a novelist and freelance copy editor. Currently she is at work on a novel and screenplay. This is her first year as a WriteGirl volunteer.

Katherine Thompson is a poet, essayist and teacher, originally from North Carolina. She is currently one of WriteGirl's In-Schools Program Coordinators. Her passions include Rainer Maria Rilke, cats, saving the Earth, the Moosewood cookbooks, farmers' markets, NPR, tarot, travel and WriteGirl!

Rachel Torres spends her days in Los Angeles working at an Internet company, reading, writing and being inspired by her very cool mentee, Jaclyn.

Marlys West is an award-winning poet and writer living in Los Angeles. She was a Hodder Fellow at Princeton University, an NEA grant recipient, and received her M.F.A. from the Michener Center for Writers. She is editing a new collection of poems and a novel.

Lindsay William-Ross has an M.A. in Creative Writing from CSULA, and worked as a Lecturer in their English Department for several years. Lindsay has been with LAist since 2005, and currently is the site's co-editor. Her work has been published in various anthologies.

After bartending in clubs in NYC, Paris and Geneva, **Rachel Wimberly** got her Master's in journalism at NYU. She started out as a producer for CNN Business News, followed by stints at *The New York Times* Regional Newspaper Group, *The New Mexican*, *Variety* and *Tradeshow Week*.

Terry Wolverton is author of seven books and editor of fourteen literary anthologies. She is the founder of Writers At Work, a creative writing center in Los Angeles, where she teaches fiction, creative nonfiction, and poetry. *www.terrywolverton.xbuild.com*

Melissa Wong is a TV writer in L.A., working on variety shows such as the MTV Movie Awards and the People's Choice Awards. She also lends her pop-culture expertise to E!'s red carpet coverage, and blogs about burgers for Examiner.com.

Natalie Zimmerman has considered herself a writer ever since she was a child. She enjoys writing screenplays, poetry, travel and children's stories. She studied screenwriting with the UCLA Professional Programs, and holds a B.A. in English and Film and Media Studies.

INDEX

S

T

V

W

Z

About the Publisher/Editor and WriteGirl Leadership

Keren Taylor, founder and Executive Director of WriteGirl, has been active as a community leader for more than 15 years. She has edited and designed dozens of anthologies and has served as publisher and editor of all of WriteGirl's award-winning books. Passionate about helping women and girls, Keren has conducted hundreds of creative writing workshops for youth and adults, and has led staff development workshops for the California Paraeducators Conference, California School-Age Consortium, California Department of Education, Los Angeles County Office of Education, LA's BEST and the New York Partnership for After School Education, among others. Keren has been selected to serve as a Community Champion and facilitator for the Annenberg Alchemy Program and is a popular speaker at conferences and book festivals nationwide including the Association of Writing Programs (AWP) Annual Conference, BOOST Conference, *Los Angeles Times* Festival of Books and Guiding Lights Festival. Keren is the recipient of numerous awards and accolades, including the President's Volunteer Call to Service Award, Business & Professional Women's Community Woman of Achievement Award, Soroptomist International's Woman of Distinction Award, commendations from Los Angeles Mayor Antonio Villaraigosa and others.

Keren is an assemblage artist and mosaicist. Her artwork has been exhibited at the The Annex LA, Barnsdall Art Center, Gallery 727, Rock Rose Gallery and Shambhala Center Los Angeles, and is in personal collections. Her assemblage works are featured on the book covers of several WriteGirl anthologies. She holds a Bachelor's Degree in International Relations from the University of British Columbia, a Piano Performance Degree from the Royal Conservatory of Music, Toronto and a Diploma from the American Music and Dramatic Academy, New York City. Keren has overseen WriteGirl's expansion into a thriving community of women and teen writers and an organization that helps hundreds of Los Angeles girls annually.

Allison Deegan serves as WriteGirl's Associate Director and has provided critical strategic and operational guidance since the organization's inception in 2001. She participates in all aspects of WriteGirl's leadership, programming and sustainability, and also serves on the WriteGirl Advisory Board. Professionally, Allison is a Business Manager with the Los Angeles County Office of Education, following a career as a marketing and financial consultant. She has made numerous presentations around the country on topics related to after-school program success, creative writing and working with youth. She is a mentor, trainer and curriculum consultant with the California School-Age Consortium, which provides professional development to after-school program staff. She holds a B.S. in Marketing from Syracuse University, a Master's degree in Public Policy from California State University, Long Beach, and is currently finishing a doctoral program in Educational Leadership, also at CSULB. Allison is a screenwriter and fiction writer who has remained close to her WriteGirl mentee, who graduated from college this spring.

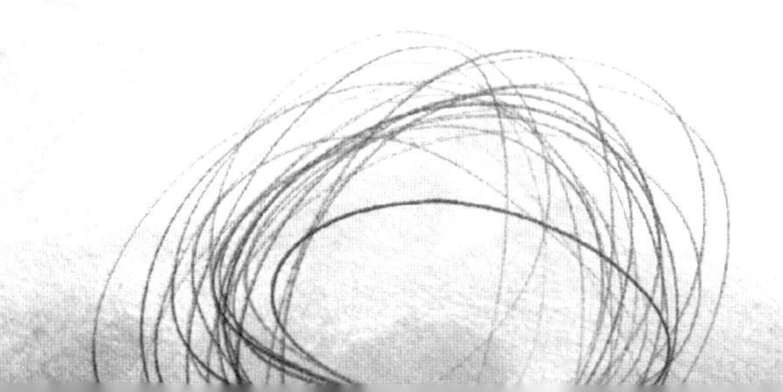

About WriteGirl

WriteGirl is a creative writing organization for teens founded in 2001 in Los Angeles. Through mentoring relationships with professional women writers, workshops, readings and publications, WriteGirl's innovative program offers girls techniques and insights in all genres of writing, helping them to develop communication skills, confidence, self-esteem and an expanded view of themselves and their futures. WriteGirl is proud to be the recipient of the Medal of Service Award from Governor Arnold Schwarzenegger and First Lady Maria Shriver as the 2010-11 California Nonprofit of the Year! WriteGirl is a project of nonprofit organization Community Partners.

Other Publications by WriteGirl

Silhouette: Bold Lines and Voices from WriteGirl
Listen to Me: Shared Secrets from WriteGirl
Lines of Velocity: Words that Move from WriteGirl
Untangled: Stories & Poetry from the Women and Girls of WriteGirl
Nothing Held Back: Truth and Fiction from WriteGirl
Pieces of Me: The Voices of WriteGirl
Bold Ink: Collected Voices of Women & Girls
Threads
Pens on Fire: Creative Writing Experiments for Teens

WriteGirl welcomes your support and involvement: visit WriteGirl on the web at www.writegirl.org

Embrace your quirkiness.